"My name is Lauren Walters. I'm a nurse here. You're on a respirator, so I know you can't talk, but do you know what happened to you?"

He nodded, watching her intently. She was very young and quite lovely. She was also watching him as carefully as he watched her. Slowly he raised a hand and made a motion like a gun.

"That's right, Mr.—I'm sorry, but you were brought in without an ID. If I get a piece of paper, do you think you could write your name?"

He nodded again, never taking his eyes from her. He felt her touch for the first time as she gently put a pencil into his fingers.

Write his name. Tell her who he was. What could be easier? He tightened his hold on the pencil. *Why couldn't he remember?*

Dear Reader,

What a lineup we have for you this month. As always, we're starting out with a bang with our Heartbreakers title, Linda Turner's *The Loner*. This tale of a burned-out ex-DEA agent and the alluring journalist who is about to uncover *all* his secrets is one you won't want to miss.

Justine Davis's *The Morning Side of Dawn* is a book readers have been asking for ever since hero Dar Cordell made his first appearance. Whether or not you've met Dar before, you'll be moved beyond words by this story of the power of love to change lives. Maura Seger's *Man Without a Memory* is a terrific amnesia book, with a hero who will enter your heart and never leave. Veteran author Marcia Evanick makes her Intimate Moments debut with *By the Light of the Moon,* a novel that proves that though things are not always what they seem, you can never doubt the truth of love. *Man of Steel* is the soul-stirring finale of Kathleen Creighton's Into the Heartland trilogy. I promise, you'll be sorry to say goodbye to the Browns. Finally, welcome new author Christa Conan, whose *All I Need* will be all *you* need to finish off another month of perfect reading.

As always, enjoy!

Yours,

Leslie Wainger
Senior Editor and Editorial Coordinator

Please address questions and book requests to:
Silhouette Reader Service
U.S.: 3010 Walden Ave., P.O. Box 1325, Buffalo, NY 14269
Canadian: P.O. Box 609, Fort Erie, Ont. L2A 5X3

MAN WITHOUT A MEMORY

MAURA SEGER

Silhouette

INTIMATE™ MOMENTS®

Published by Silhouette Books

America's Publisher of Contemporary Romance

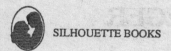

SILHOUETTE BOOKS

ISBN 0-373-07675-4

MAN WITHOUT A MEMORY

Printed in U.S.A.

MAURA SEGER

and her husband, Michael, met while they were both working for the same company. Married after a whirlwind courtship that might have been taken directly from a romance novel, Maura credits her husband's patient support and good humor for helping her fulfill the lifelong dream of being a writer. Currently writing contemporaries for Silhouette and historicals for Harlequin and mainstream, she finds that writing each book is an adventure filled with fascinating people who never fail to surprise her.

Chapter 1

There was nothing particularly remarkable about the man lying on the gurney in Trauma 3. He'd been shot three times, once in the stomach, twice in the chest. His clothes were cut off and he was hooked up to half a dozen monitors, IVs and a ventilator.

The ER team swarmed around him, their movements looking chaotic but actually well coordinated and thoroughly professional. They were doing what they'd done a thousand times before—trying to save a life.

That was complicated in this case by the fact that the guy was already dead. But then plenty of dead people showed up at St. Mary's emergency room. The losers were the ones who were still dead when they left.

This guy was going to be one of them unless he caught a major break real fast. Felix was starting to sweat. That was always a bad sign. When Felix sweated, it meant that his brain was twisting around the idea that maybe all the CPR he was doing wasn't going to work. Maybe, just maybe, he was going to have to let this one go.

"Eleven minutes," Lauren Walters said. She managed to sound matter-of-fact and regretful at the same time. She'd had enough practice. Eight years in nursing, six of them in ER and two as assistant head of ER nursing at St. Mary's, meant she'd seen pretty much everything. Too much of it tended to show up in her dreams lately, but she wasn't going to think about that just now.

Eleven minutes since CPR was begun. That didn't count the additional time in the ambulance with the medic pumping away at the guy's chest, keeping him going long enough to make it into Trauma 3 and Felix's determined hands. They already had him bagged, a breathing tube down his throat; chest X rays were coming along with blood gases and all the usual tests. But it was threatening to be academic.

She glanced at the little green-screened monitors with their readouts. Nothing. The patient was flat lining. Felix didn't have a whole lot of options left. He could crack the chest, pumping the heart directly while straddling it for the ride to OR, but that was grandstanding and, besides, everyone knew it virtually never worked. They were running out of time. Her eye caught his. He nodded. Straightening away from the table, he reached for the paddles. "Clear!"

Everyone stepped back. Felix planted the paddles, charged with enough voltage to wake the dead. An old ER joke, but one not especially funny now.

The readout jumped, spiked, went flat again. Felix was sweating worse than ever. He looked at Lauren again. She kept her eyes steady, not letting him see how far out on the edge she thought they were.

"Clear!"

Same drill. Hard thud as the volts hit, patient's back arching reflexively, white line spiking and then... Lauren held her breath, unaware that her teeth were digging into her lower lip. The guy couldn't be more than thirty, thirty-five tops. What did he want to die for, anyway? C'mon...

The line shot up again, fluttered a little and kept going. On its own.

"Hey," Felix said, looking pleased. "Whatta ya know?"

The tension in the room eased the smallest fraction, but the pace didn't slow. The patient was still a long way from the OR and the surgeons who might—just might—be able to stitch him back together.

Lauren kept her eyes on the readouts. Over the years, she'd developed a kind of sixth sense, the ability to get more out of the information the little machines provided than was the norm. That was why Felix and a lot of the other ER doctors liked having her on their tours. They thought she gave them an extra edge.

Lauren didn't know about that, but she liked what she saw. The heart was pumping blood on its own again, and less of it was ending up on the ER floor. The guy might be a winner, after all.

Twenty minutes later, when he was wheeled out for the quick trip upstairs to surgery, she let herself feel a little flicker of hope that he would make it. She was stripping off her gloves and gown, having already removed the plastic face guard, when Felix joined her. He looked happy.

"Thought he was a goner."

Lauren nodded. "Tough one."

"Y'never know, sometimes they surprise you. Any ID on him?"

Felix had a natural urge to know the name of the man whose life they had just saved . . . maybe.

"I don't know," Lauren said. "I'll take a look. He ought to have a wallet or something." She was turning back to Trauma 3, where orderlies were already cleaning up the mess, when the nurse on the desk called out.

"Four-car collision over on Fifth. They're bringing them in now. Looks bad."

Even as she spoke, ambulance sirens wailed outside. Felix grabbed clean gloves and raced for the doors. Lauren did the same. Somebody else would have to find out who the man was.

Sweet Lord, her neck hurt. Third time this week, the same throbbing pain that felt like somebody was twisting a knife right between the first and second cervical vertebrae. It was stress, of course, but knowing that didn't make it hurt any less.

Lauren ran down the list of medications she could take—for the umpteenth time—while she eased her sweater on over her head. The women's locker room was quiet. She'd stayed on for an hour past shift change to help out with a cardiac fibrillation.

It was after midnight. She was due back on at eight. Like so many hospitals, St. Mary's was short on nurses. The powers-that-be had decided against hiring any more, preferring to work the ones they had into the ground. Lauren sighed. She hadn't been looking for a cushy berth when she signed on, but this was getting ridiculous.

Maybe she would have to think about that corporate job she'd been offered, taking blood pressures and running physicals on harried executives at a Fortune 500 company three blocks and a universe away from St. Mary's. It was more money and a whole lot less aggravation.

The only problem was that she figured she would be dead of boredom in about a week. Really dead, not the bring 'em back alive variety she and her colleagues specialized in.

She was grinning at the thought as she left the locker room, picturing herself and Felix riding around on some demented frontier lassoing patients before they could stumble into the great beyond. The idea had an almost hallucinatory quality to it. She really needed to get some sleep soon or she was going to be a candidate for—

"Hey, Lauren."

It was Ginny Germaine, head night nurse on ER, whippet thin, honed for action, black coffee in her veins. Perfect for the job. Lauren gave her a tired wave as she passed the desk.

"Hey, Ginny. I'm outta here."

Ginny laughed, her bright smile flashing in her cocoa brown face. "Try an' get some sleep, girl. You got bags under your bags."

"You're just saying that to make me feel better."

"That's true. Hey, heard you saved that guy got shot over on Park this afternoon. He made the *Trib*'s front page."

Lauren glanced down at the tabloid lying on the desk. There was a large black-and-white photo of a man in a business suit lying on the sidewalk next to an expensive-looking sports car. The headline blared JOHN DOE: 500th Shooting Victim This Year...And Counting.

The paper was on yet another antiviolence crusade.

"No ID on him?" Lauren asked, mildly curious. She was too tired for anything more than that.

Ginny shrugged. "Guess not. Somebody'll know him, though, a good-looking man like that."

Lauren glanced at the photo again. For the first time, she noticed that the man who had lain before her naked in the emergency room was more than simply a collection of terrible injuries and faltering vital signs. He was also undeniably handsome. Not even the grainy quality of the photo or the fact that he was unconscious when it was taken could change that.

Thick dark hair framed a face that might have been lifted straight off the statue of a Greek god. His eyes were closed, dark lashes dusting his cheeks. His nose was straight, his mouth chiseled, his chin firm. He looked extremely fit and she remembered Felix saying that the guy was in peak condition as he worked on him, as though daring him to be in that good shape and still die over a little thing like three bullets tearing up his insides.

"He made it through surgery?" she asked, suddenly caring in a way that she didn't usually let herself because it hurt too damn much. God, she really was tired.

Ginny nodded.

"He's in ICU. They got a cop parked there with him." The older nurse grimaced. She'd worked ICU for several years and, like everyone else, complained when the cops got underfoot, but not very much. There were times when having a cop around was definitely a good thing.

"Glad he made it," Lauren said. She was starting to hear a buzz in her ears.

Ginny took another look at her and shook her head. "Honey, you better go home now or we're gonna have to check you in."

Now there was truth for you, Lauren thought. Rather than submit herself to the tender mercies of St. Mary's, she headed for the door. When she'd arrived for work seventeen plus hours before, it had been a pleasant early spring day. Now it was dark, cold and raining. Perfect.

She sighed, pulled her jacket more tightly around herself and, head down, hurried along the street. The reflected glow of street lamps shone in puddles cast up by passing cars. She dodged one, glared at the driver who ignored her and went on.

It was her luck—whether good or bad, she couldn't decide—to have an apartment in a building owned by the hospital less than a block away. Granted, it was just a tiny studio with paper-thin walls and questionable plumbing, but she could actually afford it and she didn't have to spend hours commuting like so many of her friends.

Of course, it also meant that whenever a hole had to be plugged on the nursing schedule, who did the hospital call? Good ol' Lauren, of course, who lived only a block away and couldn't seem to say no to overtime.

Maybe it was past time she learned. She let herself into the lobby with its too-bright overhead fluorescent lights and punched the button for the elevator. When the door slid open, she jerked awake, abruptly aware that she'd been dozing. Hey, she had a bed for that.

Upstairs, she fumbled with the key in the door, finally got it open and lurched inside, just managing to lock the door behind her. The temptation to sleep in her clothes was almost overwhelming, but she knew from hard-won experience how awful she would feel in the morning.

Staying awake under a warm shower wasn't easy, but she managed it. She even remembered to shampoo her thankfully short auburn hair. It was still almost as fine and curly as when she was a child, and dried quickly as a result.

Not that it mattered. It could have stayed sopping wet and she wouldn't have cared. Her head touched the pillow. In the next breath, she was asleep.

The dream came as it always had, seeming perfectly ordinary, nothing to be alarmed about. Not a nightmare at all.

She was in the hospital, just going on duty in the ER. It was daytime. There was the usual bustle, people coming and going, mountains of paperwork to be shoveled, but nothing alarming. Just another day on the job.

Then it changed. There were screams nearby. A child, maybe, she couldn't be sure. Someone terrified and in agony, and a doctor cursing with that note of fear in the voice that says the battle's being lost.

She had to get to them, had to help, but she couldn't seem to move. She was frozen in place, the screams tearing through her and everyone else floating past, hearing nothing, even laughing. Laughing at her, and pointing because she was stuck to the floor, paralyzed, hardly breathing while the screams went on and on.

No, not stuck. She was on a gurney, propped upright against a wall so that everyone could see her, with tubes stuck in and the straps holding her down. Trapped. With a wrenching effort, she tore free and ran down the corridor that split the two sides of the ER, still hearing the screams, looking in one room after another, trying to find whoever needed help.

All the rooms were full, but the people in them were dead, except they could still sit up and laugh at her as she kept running, sobbing now, her chest hurting, until she ran straight into the curtains that hung down from the ceiling. They wrapped around her, suffocatingly close. She slapped at them but they got thicker, tighter. She couldn't get out, couldn't breathe, and still the screams went on and on....

And on... Her screams, her own voice, shocked her awake. She sat up with a jerk. Her heart was slamming against her rib cage and her breath came in sobs. She was afraid she was going to vomit.

In the bathroom, she flicked on the light and stared at herself in the small mirror above the sink. The woman who gazed back at her was white-faced with

wide, cornflower blue eyes and a smattering of freck-
les across her nose that looked unnaturally dark against
the paleness of her skin.

At twenty-eight, she could easily pass for ten years
younger than that and still routinely got carded when
she went out with friends. But tonight—no, not night,
it was morning now—no one would have mistaken her
for anything other than what she was, a too-tired, too-
stressed woman with too much on her mind. So much,
in fact, that the sleep that should have been her relief
was becoming an unbearable torment instead.

Wearily, she shook her head. It made no sense that
this was happening to her now. Nothing had changed
in her life. It was exactly the same as it had been for
years.

She'd always worked hard. There'd been no other
way out of a rundown midwestern factory town where
the factories had all shut down and the future turned
ugly. So many of the people she'd grown up with were
still there, living in the clapboard row houses with their
peeling paint and air of hopelessness. Or they were in
jail; she knew a few like that. Or they were dead.

Not her. She'd always wanted more, and the changes
she'd seen coming had only spurred her on. She'd gotten out, but she hadn't forgotten. Remembering was
part of what made her a good nurse, or at least it had.
Lately, it seemed memory had become her worst enemy.

She ran a hand over her face and grimaced. There
were people she could go see. The hospital kept such
services available. It was all free and confidential, a

remarkable generosity that signaled how very serious the problem could be.

But the thought of sitting in an office, talking about her deepest, darkest feelings made her shudder. Maybe she could find some other way.

Back in the bedroom, she glanced at the clock. It was after five o'clock. There was no point going to bed again and risking another nightmare.

She went into the tiny kitchen and began making breakfast, concentrating on every small task. If she did that, if she just paid attention to exactly what she had to do, maybe she could keep herself from thinking about anything else.

Then all she would have to do was find a way not to have to sleep. The sheer simplicity of that made her laugh. And laugh and laugh until she heard herself and stopped abruptly, a hand clamped over her mouth.

Chapter 2

He couldn't scream. He wanted to, the urge was irresistible, but there was something in his throat preventing him. The only sound he could make was a faint gurgling moan. It wasn't really enough to convince him he was alive.

He could see—what? There was a gray darkness all around, begrudging him just enough light to make out a few indeterminable shapes that gave him no clue to where he was.

He could hear beeping, a persistent, high-pitched beeping that he realized had been going on for a long time without him being aware. It sounded urgent, but, again, told him nothing.

He could smell sharp odors he couldn't identify, not unpleasant exactly, but not anything that made him feel warm and fuzzy, either.

Maybe this was hell. A strange kind of hell where he could feel incredible pain searing all around the edges of him, but somehow he didn't care. There was a thick, soft wall of sorts between him and the pain, not solid enough to keep him from knowing that the pain was there, but making it seem almost as though it was happening to someone else.

Except it wasn't. On that much he was clear. It was him in the shadowy darkness with the damn beeping and the smells. Him with the thing down his throat and the pain.

An image flashed through his mind, the blurred shape of a man holding a gun. He felt a jolt of disbelief and knew he was remembering, knew the gun was pointed at him. Knew it was going off.

He still couldn't scream, but he damn well tried.

"I hate to do this to you," Martha Morrissey said, "but I've got one nurse out with pneumonia, another broke her ankle and a third's got the mother of all cases of morning sickness. That leaves us up the creek in ICU. If you could just do one shift..." The nursing supervisor looked at Lauren beseechingly.

"I've been putting in a lot of overtime—"

"I know and we really appreciate it. But we're in an awful bind and I'm counting on you."

"If we hired more nurses, this wouldn't happen."

Martha grimaced. "Oh, God, don't you think I know that? Not a week goes by that I don't complain to the board about the staffing situation. You know what they say? They tell me they'd rather pay overtime than add overhead. We can't hire anyone, but the patients still keep coming and they have to be cared for. I worked three extra shifts myself last week in obstetrics, pediatrics and OR, plus doing all the usual administrative crap. And I've got three kids, a husband who's screaming and parents who want me to help them move to Florida. C'mon, Lauren, gimme a break.''

If Martha Morrissey had been one of the uptight, rule-book administrators that Lauren had encountered from time to time, she just might have told her to shove off. But Martha was one of the good guys. She really did pitch in whenever and wherever she could, and she cared about her nurses. She had the ulcer to prove it.

''Okay, okay, I'll work the shift. ICU, you said?''

Martha gave her a relieved smile. ''You're gonna love it. It's practically empty up there right now. Can you believe that?''

''What happened, everybody suddenly get better?''

''Hey, enjoy it while you can. It won't last.''

No, Lauren thought as she waited for the elevator to take her upstairs, it wouldn't. If there was one thing she and everyone else at St. Mary's could count on, it was a steady stream of customers.

But the ICU was quieter than usual. Stepping onto the floor, she was struck by how peaceful it was compared to the ER. Except for two nurses and a resident talking quietly among themselves at the desk, nothing seemed to be going on.

Or at least that was how it looked until she noticed the cop sitting outside one of the rooms. Oh, yes, Mr. Doe. Ignoring the little rush of pleasure she felt at knowing he was still alive, Lauren went over to the desk. It was time to get to work.

The darkness had faded. It was brighter now. He could make out shapes better. There was an empty chair close enough that he could have reached out and touched it, assuming that he could move his arm, which he didn't seem able to manage. There was also a box on wheels, the source of the beeping sound. Some sort of equipment. It appeared to be hooked up to him.

Hospital. He'd been shot and he was now in a hospital. The realization flooded into him. For just a second, he felt a surge of panic, but he forced it down. If he was in the hospital, he was doing okay. And if he just kept telling himself that, maybe it would be true.

This wasn't a regular room. There were no windows, just clear walls that looked out into a bigger space that seemed surrounded by other rooms like the one he was in. People were moving around on the other side of those walls.

One of them was coming in his direction. A nurse. She paused to speak to someone he couldn't see, then entered the room. Lifting a chart from the bottom of the bed, she studied it.

He waited. A moment or two passed. She glanced up and saw him watching her. A surprised smile lit up her face.

"Hey, you're back," she said.

He tried to nod, and almost managed it.

"That's great. You're in the intensive care unit in St. Mary's Hospital in New York. My name is Lauren Walters. I'm a nurse here. You were brought in last

night and required surgery. Right now you're on a
ventilator so I know you can't talk, but do you know
what happened to you?''

He nodded, watching her intently. She was very
young and quite lovely. She was also watching him as
carefully as he watched her. Slowly, he raised a hand,
gratified that he could do so, and made a motion like
a gun.

"That's right, Mr.—I'm sorry, but you were brought
in without an ID. If I get a piece of paper, do you think
you could write your name?"

He nodded again, never taking his eyes from her. She
fished in her pocket, found a piece of paper and
smoothed it out on the bed beside his hand. He felt her
touch for the first time as she gently put a pencil into
his fingers.

Write his name. Tell them who he was. What could
be easier? He tightened his hold on the pencil. Why
couldn't he—?

"What's wrong?" Lauren asked.

He shook his head, feeling the panic again, struggling to fight it.

She laid a hand gently on his shoulder. "It's okay,
just relax. You've been through a lot. Let's not push
it." She took the paper and pencil back, slid them away
in her pocket. "I'm going to tell the doctor you're
conscious. She'll be in to see you soon."

The smile she gave him this time was strictly professional. She turned and hurried from the room.

"Problem?" the young cop asked. He straightened
slightly in his chair.

Lauren shook her head. "Nothing unusual," she said and brushed past him. Maybe that was even true. Plenty of patients who had gone through what John Doe had experienced all sorts of side effects, including varying degrees of confusion. But she'd seen something in his face when he tried to write his name that warned her there might be more to it than that.

Protocol said she had to check with the ICU resident first, but she was busy with one of the car accident victims from the night before. Instead, Lauren picked up the phone and paged surgery. Pat Merkle was on call. She hadn't done the work on Mr. Doe, but she was good. If there was any problem, she would spot it.

"We're going to try taking you off the ventilator, sir," Pat said, three hours later. John Doe had been checked from stem to stern—X rays, blood gases, EEG, everything. For a man who had been on his way to eternity only the night before, he was doing remarkably well.

"Wilson's got a nice touch," Pat said in an aside to Lauren. The surgeon was referring to her colleague who had done the stitching on John Doe. He'd been called, and agreed that all the signs indicated the patient could resume breathing on his own.

"The procedure is slightly uncomfortable," Pat went on, "but it isn't painful and it won't take long."

Lauren stood by, ready to assist. But Pat had a nice touch of her own. She had the tube out and the stethoscope to Mr. Doe's chest in record time.

"Nice," she murmured after a few moments of listening to him breathe. "You have two functioning lungs again. I know they may not feel exactly like that, but they are working."

She straightened up and turned to Lauren. "Okay, here's what I think we need to do."

As the discussion wrapped up, Pat drew Lauren aside. Quietly, so as not to be overheard, she said, "If this thing about his name keeps up, call Litzer in neurology. Have him take a look."

Lauren nodded. "It's probably nothing."

"The guy was practically DOA, Lauren. How long did Felix have to work on him?"

"Eleven minutes." Funny how she remembered that. She didn't usually.

Pat shrugged. "Maybe he's fine, but call Litzer if you have any doubts."

Unspoken between them was the knowledge that despite everything Felix and the rest of the team had done, brain damage was a possibility. The mere thought made Lauren's stomach twist.

Pat went on to other things, leaving Lauren to give her full attention to Mr. Doe. His eyes were closed. She thought he might have slipped into a natural sleep and hoped that was the case, but as she bent over him, his eyes opened suddenly.

"What did you—" His voice was low and rasping, the result of having had a tube down his throat. He stopped, looking surprised.

"It's okay," Lauren said quickly. "Your throat's going to be sore for a while but I can get you something for that."

He shook his head emphatically. "I'm doped enough." Every word was a struggle but he was clearly determined to get them out. "What did you say your name is?"

"Lauren Walters. Care to tell me yours?"

He made a sound that could have been a laugh. "I'd love to, but there's just one problem."

"You can't remember?"

"Tell me you gave me some drug that does that."

"Actually, you've had about a zillion drugs shot through you since last night and, in combination, they can cause all sorts of things to happen. Why don't you just try to relax for a while and we'll see if it comes to you?"

He sure didn't sound brain damaged, Lauren thought as she left the room. Exhausted, ill and confused, yes, but not brain damaged.

All the same, if his memory didn't return soon, she would have to call Litzer.

"John Doe's awake?" the cop asked as she came out. He was on his feet, looking into the room.

"Yes, he is, but—"

"Good, I gotta call in. A couple of detectives want to talk with him."

"I'm not sure how much he'll be able to tell you. Besides, he has to be cleared by the doctor before he can have visitors."

The cop frowned. "I thought a doc was just in there."

"She was, but she didn't say anything about visitors." Bless Pat for leaving that out. Lauren had the strong notion that their mystery guest would appreciate a little time to himself, at least until he could get his thoughts in order.

"He must remember something," the policeman insisted. "Don't you think he'd want us to get whoever did this to him?"

The cop had a point. If somebody had put three of their best slugs in her, Lauren would sure as hell want them caught. "I'll ask the doctor about visitors," she promised.

"Could you do that soon? It's been almost a day already. The longer we wait, the less chance there is of us getting anyone."

"The trail gets cold?" Lauren asked. She'd heard that on TV.

"Yeah, maybe, but you know how it is—another day, another dozen or so shootings. You kinda get pushed to the rear, you know?"

Kind of like in the ER, she thought, where you did what you could for whoever happened to be in front of you, then went on to the next one and the next and didn't look back.

"He's a little confused," Lauren said, "but I'll see what I can do."

"What's his name, by the way?"

"Uh, I didn't get it. Like I said, he's confused."

The cop gave her a sharp look. "He doesn't know his name?"

"He can barely talk, Officer. We just took him off the ventilator. Why not give him a little time to get used to the idea that he's still alive?"

"Yeah, okay, but whatever you can do—"

Lauren assured him she would get on it right away. Pat had been on her way into surgery; she wouldn't be available again for several hours. Wilson wasn't due back on until four o'clock. Maybe by then, Mr. Doe would be remembering who he was.

And who had tried to kill him.

He couldn't remember his name. It wasn't Rumpelstiltskin, he was sure of that. But it could be just about anything else—Tom, Dick, Harry…Juan, Pierre, Woo Lee…anything. Hell, he had no idea what he looked like. With enormous effort, he managed to raise a hand high enough to see it.

His skin was white. Not white-white but kind of swarthy with dark hair on the arm. He could have been anything from Hispanic to Italian to Arab. Except he was thinking in English and he was pretty sure that came naturally to him.

Okay, so he was American and Caucasian and male. There couldn't be more than fifty, sixty million guys like that. Figuring out which one he was ought to be a cinch.

How could he not know his name? That was so basic, what could possibly have caused him to lose it?

But then he'd lost a few other things, too. His wallet, if he understood things right. The pretty young nurse said he'd come in with no ID. Surely, there would have been something in his wallet.

Then there was the little matter of almost losing his life. His head was clear enough now that he could breathe on his own, but he was still getting the message that he'd come real close to going off the edge. He was in intensive care, after all. They didn't put you in there because they liked you.

Somebody had tried to kill him. He'd faced that person, looked right at him and seen—

The gun. He could still see it quite clearly. A 9 millimeter Smith & Wesson equipped with a silencer. Not your usual Saturday night special. But behind it was...nothing. Or almost nothing. Just a dark blur that was probably a person, but could have been a really talented gorilla, for all he knew.

He took a deep breath and groaned. The doctor had assured him his lungs were both working. Easy for her to say. Still, he would go a long way before he let them put him on that tube again.

A movement by the glass walls caught his eye. He turned his head slightly and found himself looking into the face of a cop. The immediate thought that went through his mind was as illuminating as it was obscene.

Whoever he was, he didn't like cops.

This one looked as though he was thinking about coming in for a little chat. Rather than have that happen, John Doe turned his head away and closed his eyes.

He would just rest a little, then think some more. Maybe even try to sit up. He could manage that, he thought. He'd better. Hanging around the hospital very long might not be the best idea.

Somebody had tried to kill him. Somebody who was still out there and who just might decide to finish the job.

Chapter 3

"Let me make sure I understand this," the detective said. "You didn't see the guy who shot you, you have no idea why anyone would want to do such a thing and you don't know who you are or why you happen to be in New York, even whether you live here or not. Is that right?"

"That's it," John said.

Lauren had started thinking of him as John. She wasn't comfortable with just *he* or *him*. He was a human being and a patient. He needed a name.

But he sure wasn't coming up with one on his own.

The detective shut his notebook. He cleared his throat. "I'd like permission to take your fingerprints, sir."

"Why?"

"To identify you."

"I'd have had to already be fingerprinted for that to work."

The detective nodded. "That's right, but since you don't know who you are, you don't know if your fingerprints are on record or not. We could find out."

John hesitated. He smiled slightly, as though he liked the detective and thought he was doing a very conscientious job. He just wasn't necessarily going to cooperate.

"I'll think about it."

"I don't see why you'd have to, sir. After all, it's in your own best interest to establish your identity, isn't it?"

The smile deepened. It was really extraordinary how he could smile like that less than forty-eight hours after getting shot and while still lying in the ICU. Although he probably wouldn't be there much longer. Wilson was looking to move him to post-op in another day or so if he kept doing so well.

Meanwhile, Lauren was back working another extra shift on ICU, this time only partly at Martha's behest. She told herself it wasn't such a big deal, that she was just curious about John Doe. Taking a personal interest in a patient occasionally wasn't a crime. She would just be careful not to overdo it.

Besides, she had the definite feeling that he was going to be a favorite on post-op. Once he was there, she probably wouldn't be able to get near him.

Not that she cared particularly. Not at all. She was just struck by his courage—he didn't complain or protest or do anything to suggest he was in any discomfort. But he had to be hurting, especially since he'd insisted on tapering off the pain medication.

"The neurologist I spoke with indicated he believed my memory would return soon and that it would be better to just let that happen," John told the detective pleasantly.

That was true; Litzer had said it. But he'd also told Lauren privately that in twelve years of practicing neurology, he'd never before seen a genuine case of amnesia. But he thought he was seeing one now.

John Doe fit the profile down the line—heavy-duty trauma, big-time medications. The textbooks said to leave him alone. His memory would return soon, but efforts to rush it could cause problems.

She was on the verge of telling the detective that herself when he closed his notebook and prepared to leave. He looked like a man who had tried as much as he figured he could. Now he had to move on.

"Okay, sir. If you change your mind or if you happen to remember anything about whoever it was who tried to kill you, let us know."

"I'm assuming it was a random street thing," John said.

"Yeah, maybe, but then you're not in much of a position to assume anything. Here's my card." He dropped it on the table beside the bed and left.

When he was gone, John took a deep breath. His features became more relaxed. Up until then, Lauren hadn't noticed how tense he was around the detective. In the back of her mind, she wondered why. But she had more immediate concerns.

"Your vital signs are great," she told him. "There's talk about moving you out of here."

"Sounds good to me."

"You'll love post-op. They actually let you eat there."

"Hospital food?"

" 'Fraid so, but it's not anywhere near as bad as it used to be. They test it on us first. Of course, that's not the same thing as testing it on humans, but—"

He laughed, winced and shook his head. "I've got to stop doing that. Seriously, how much longer am I going to be here?"

"In ICU? Another day, maybe two."

"No, I mean in the hospital. I shouldn't need much more time, right?"

Lauren swallowed her surprise. There was a belief among doctors and nurses that the best possible sign of a patient's recovery was that same patient griping about wanting out of the hospital. But this was ridiculous.

Was it possible Mr. Doe really didn't understand how badly hurt he'd been? For that matter, still was?

"It's a little premature to be thinking about releasing you," she said. "Especially with the memory loss you're experiencing."

"I'll get over that."

If the steely look in his eyes was anything to go by, his conviction was guaranteed. Not for the first time since he'd regained consciousness, she was struck by the particular quality of light in his eyes. They were an unusual shade of gray in contrast to the midnight darkness of his hair. Hair that was very well cut for all that it was rumpled.

Against the whiteness of the hospital sheets, his chest appeared bronzed and heavily muscled with a light dusting of dark curls. They were going to love that chest in post-op, Lauren mused.

On impulse, she reached out and turned his hand over. There were calluses on the palm and on the inside of the knuckles as though he'd spent a lot of time gripping something hard. She checked the other hand. They were there, too.

"That's interesting."

"What is?"

"Your hands are callused, but in an unusual way. I've seen it before, but I can't quite place it."

His smile was brilliantly white against several days' growth of beard. "A clue?"

"Could be. The way people live tends to etch itself onto their bodies. For example, it's a common misconception that people who do a lot of physical labor tend to be in good overall condition. Generally, they show muscular development in certain areas and simple wear-and-tear everywhere else. But in your case—"

In his case, the muscular development was perfectly and evenly distributed all over his body. Either he spent a tremendous amount of time in the gym or—

"Maybe you're an athlete. Do you feel a powerful desire to pick up a tennis racket?"

He frowned, thinking it over. "I've got an idea I've played tennis, but nothing more than that."

"It was just a thought. We'll figure it out. In the meantime, you really have to get some rest."

That he agreed with only a slight protest told her he must be exhausted. Lauren slipped out of the room. She was on duty another two hours, but John did not wake again.

She was gone. He'd awakened with the thought that he would see her only to find that she was off duty. In her place was a perfectly nice, perfectly competent nurse he tried his best not to resent.

Lauren, that was her name. Lauren Walters. She wasn't as young as she looked, which was a relief, because at first glance he'd thought she was about twenty. Now he realized she was closer to thirty. Closer to his own age.

How did he know that? Probing lightly, he tested his memory. How old was he? A number popped into his head—thirty-four. And a date—October 16. His birthday.

Maybe. He couldn't be sure, but the chance that he was remembering something about himself filled him with hope. If he could remember his age, surely his name wasn't too far off? He probed his mind a little harder, trying, but felt as though he was running up against a peculiarly spongy wall that seemed to give but didn't.

So much for that. He would be better off thinking about Ms. Lauren Walters. The corners of his mouth lifted. He hurt like hell, more so since he'd insisted they stop doping him.

But the thought of Lauren was enough to tell him something else about himself. He might not like cops but he definitely liked women, especially auburn-haired ones with big blue eyes and cautious smiles.

Which was all well and good but didn't help him with his current situation. He hadn't been entirely honest with the detective. He remembered the gun, but he didn't see what telling him would accomplish. There had to be thousands of 9 millimeter Smith & Wessons in New York. The silencer made it a little unusual, but not all that much.

Abruptly, it occurred to him that being able to identify the gun was unusual in itself. Probably not everyone could do that. He hadn't thought about it before, but now that he did, it seemed as though he had a certain amount of knowledge about guns. Enough to recognize one particular kind when it was pointed at him.

Interesting, but again not all that helpful.

Why hadn't he let himself be fingerprinted? The excuse he'd given—about wanting to remember naturally was bogus. Moreover, the detective had known that. He'd let it show in his eyes. They could have checked his prints and simply not told him what they found out, but used the information to contact relatives, family, whoever.

Which brought him to another point—what kind of family did he have? Was he, for instance, married?

He tested the idea out, turning it over in his mind. It didn't feel right. The tennis thing had, at least a little. He wasn't a professional tennis player by any means, but he'd held a racket in his time.

What he hadn't done was get married. Or if he had, he sure didn't remember, not even a little. The mere notion of being married seemed completely foreign. Moreover, there was no sign of a ring on his left hand. Or any rings for that matter. Nothing with a school insignia, for instance, that might have given him a clue to his identity.

It would come back to him. He had to believe that just as he had to believe that he was going to get better fast and get out of the hospital.

And go where?

An image flashed through his mind. A cabin in the mountains somewhere, a wisp of smoke rising from the chimney. He was swept by a sense of peace and happiness, of... home.

Was that where he lived? Some rustic cabin in the back of beyond? He supposed it was possible. Certainly, it didn't feel entirely wrong like the marriage thing. But neither did it fit completely, either.

Still, the image of the cabin lingered, offering an odd sort of comfort as the day dragged on and he waited for Lauren to return.

She did, but not until the following morning.

"I'm back on ER full-time," Lauren explained. "I just came up to see how you're doing."

"Is that where you work usually?" John asked. It felt good to see her. Too good. He would be a fool to forget that he was strictly passing through.

Lauren nodded. "That's why I was there when you were brought in. Something occurred to me. You didn't have a wallet, but you were certainly wearing clothes. Some thoughtful soul bagged them."

She'd found them down in a storage room next to the morgue, as though put there in anticipation of their owner's arrival, but she wasn't about to tell him that.

"My clothes," John said. "That's a great idea. Let's take a look."

Lauren opened the bag and drew out the items carefully. "They're in pretty bad shape," she warned. "Besides being soaked with blood, we had to cut them off you. I hope you won't mind, but I went through the pockets. There was nothing except some loose change, a set of keys and a handkerchief, unfortunately not monogrammed."

"Nothing else?" John asked. "No address book, receipts, not even a scrap of lint?"

Lauren shook her head. "Nothing. Either you're incredibly neat or—"

"Or what?"

She hesitated, wondering exactly how much she should say. "I wondered if maybe someone had cleaned out your pockets, but I don't see how that could have happened. According to the article in the newspaper, witnesses to the shooting said the gunman fled immediately. He was so fast no one could even give a decent description of him. For sure, he didn't stop long enough to empty your pockets."

"But they were practically empty."

Lauren nodded. "I'm sure there's some explanation. Do the clothes ring a bell at all?"

John stared at them. He'd been wearing a white button-down dress shirt, a dark blue suit and a striped silk tie. Almost every inch of them was covered in dried blood, but he could still make out the labels.

"Looks like I've got expensive taste." Extremely expensive. The suit had a label in it from Savile Row, the shirt was French and the tie appeared to have come from a shop in Milan.

"Maybe you travel a lot," Lauren said. She had noticed the labels herself and been struck by what they appeared to suggest. John Doe—whoever he really was—had all the trappings of a highly successful international business executive.

But how could such a man be shot down on a New York City street and no one come forward to identify him? His picture had been splashed across the front page of the newspaper. Granted, it probably wasn't the best likeness, but surely someone should have recognized him.

Even if he wasn't from this area, he would have been in New York for a reason, perhaps for business meetings. Why did no one miss him, ask where he was, call the police?

"Strange, isn't it?" John said, as though he had read her thoughts.

"Am I that transparent?"

He laughed and this time it didn't seem to hurt as much. "Let's just say you have a very expressive face."

She glanced away, worried suddenly about what he might be seeing. There was a fine line between concern for a patient and personal interest. Lauren had never crossed it, never even been tempted. But suddenly she could see that line and knew she was getting perilously close to it.

"What about the keys?" she asked, determined to keep their attention where it belonged. The need was to get him better, both in mind and in body. Nothing else was legitimate.

He shot her a reproving smile that made her toes curl, then turned the keys over in his hand, studying them. "I'd say this one belongs to a car." He looked at it more carefully. "BMW, nice. These two look like house keys. This one—" He selected the smallest, the only one in the set that had a chrome finish rather than brass. "What do you make of this one?"

There was something vaguely familiar about it, but Lauren couldn't place it. "A mailbox?" she suggested.

"Could be. Looks a little big for that. How about a post-office box?"

"That's possible. There's a number on it."

John nodded. "Number 365. It would have to be a pretty big post office to have that many boxes."

"What about a bank?" Lauren asked suddenly. It had taken her a few moments to place it, but now she realized that the key looked very much like the one she had for her own safety deposit box. It was a year or more since she'd had any reason to use it, hence her difficulty remembering. But the more she thought about it, the more she wondered if that wasn't the answer.

John held the key up, turning it over in the light. "Could be, but which bank? There's nothing on here to indicate that."

"No, there wouldn't be. Unless you happen to remember, I'm afraid it won't do any good."

He put the keys down on the bedside table along with the handkerchief. Only the loose change remained.

"American," he said, sorting through it. "Except for this." He held up a small coin, different from all the others.

"What is it?" Lauren asked.

"Seems to be a Colombian ten-peso piece."

"Then you've been to Colombia, probably recently." She couldn't restrain a note of excitement. That was a real clue, something that might actually be traceable.

"Let's say you came back to New York, you would have gone through customs at JFK airport. A lot of places videotape arriving passengers now. If they do that there—"

"It would take days to go through all the tapes, presuming anyone was willing to do it and, besides, this could have been in my pocket for months, if not weeks."

He glanced at the coin briefly, then lay back against the pillows. "I appreciate your help, but I'm feeling rather tired now."

Lauren hesitated. She knew she was being dismissed and was more than a little concerned by how much that hurt. But beyond it was the sense that he was asking her to leave for reasons that had nothing to do with his being tired. He certainly hadn't seemed that way until just now.

Still, he had a perfect right to be alone if that was what he preferred.

His eyes were still closed, his expression unreadable. Lauren slipped out of the room. At the door, she glanced back. He looked as though he might be asleep. But the Colombian coin remained in his hand. As she watched, his finger moved over it, as though attempting to trace whatever pattern it might reveal.

Chapter 4

It couldn't have been a French franc or a Bahraini dinar, a German mark or a Chinese yuan. It had to be a peso—from Colombia.

Lauren was just coming back on duty at the ER after catching a shower and a few hours' sleep. She had roughly a thousand things she needed to be thinking about, but instead she was still focused on that damn coin.

If there was one thing her years of nursing had taught her, it was the pitfalls of stereotyping. She viewed it as the shortest possible route to the wrong conclusions, so she wasn't going to do it now. There could be any number of reasons for visiting Colombia. Maybe he'd gone to visit relatives, to do some totally legitimate business, to have a little vacation.

But then there was the unfortunate matter of the country's image, at least in the eyes of the media. Like it or not, fairly or not, Colombia was probably more associated with drug trafficking than just about any other country on earth.

Which didn't mean for a minute that John had anything to do with that. Still, he'd been there. And he obviously had money—or some way of paying for his expensive tastes. And he'd gotten shot.

And he hadn't wanted the police to fingerprint him.

Adding all that up made Lauren feel queasy. She put a hand to her stomach just as she walked past the ER nursing desk.

"Something wrong?" Ginny Germaine asked. She shot Lauren a concerned look.

"No, I'm fine. You're on again?"

Ginny shrugged. "Honey, I'm starting to forget what my apartment looks like. If something doesn't happen soon to change things—"

"I know, it's getting crazy. I hate to say it, but I think it's getting time for the union to put on a whole lot more pressure than it has so far."

"Be careful who you say that to. It could be the quickest way to getting yourself fired."

"I'm not so sure that would be the worst thing that could happen to me."

Ginny shook her head. "You're just talking like this 'cause you're tired. We all are. I heard Martha told the powers-that-be that unless they hire more people soon, they could see the death rate at this hospital notch up a couple of points at least. She let them know that was the kind of thing that could make it into the newspapers real fast."

"She really said that?"

"So I hear. They're more likely to worry about their public image than they are about any of us, so we might as well take advantage of it. Besides, Martha told them the truth. We both know there are too many corners getting cut."

"I know," Lauren agreed. "There have been times lately when I've really held my breath."

"We've been lucky so far, but that isn't going to last. Did you know they've even refused to hire more security? And they told the guards we do have that they could forget about any kind of raise."

Lauren shook her head, dismayed. "That's crazy. This is not the world's best neighborhood and, besides, there are nights when we seem to be the magnet for every loony-tune in town. They shouldn't be skimping on security any more than they should be on nursing."

"Tell them that, girl. Better yet, hope nothing happens to make them realize too late what they should have been doing all along."

Lauren nodded. She was just coming on and already she felt tired—and at least mildly depressed. For the first time in her nursing career, she was really beginning to wonder why she did what she did.

"By the way," Ginny said, interrupting her thoughts. "Your friend had a phone call."

"What do you mean?"

"Mr. Doe up in ICU. My niece, Mandy, who works at Patient Information, said somebody called yesterday asking how he was doing."

"He asked for him by name?"

"No, just said he wanted to know about the guy whose picture was on the front page of the *Trib* the other day."

"What did Mandy tell him?"

"That he'd have to be more precise, like give her a name. She explained that we've got four John Does in this hospital right now and she wasn't going to try to figure out which was which. What she didn't say, except to me, was that she would have done it if the guy had seemed to be family or a friend, but since he wouldn't even give his name, let alone the patient's, she didn't feel right about telling him anything."

"Smart woman. You think it was just some bozo?"

"Probably, town's full of them, isn't it? Anyway, about half an hour later, another guy calls up, says he's the reporter for the *Trib*, gives his name and asks for an update on your John Doe. Tells her the date he was brought in, even the time. Now that did sound more legit so she told him what she's allowed to, namely that Mr. Doe was listed as stable, but afterward she got to thinking that she should have told him to call the media office."

"If he was from the *Trib*, they would have known him there."

Ginny frowned. "You think maybe he wasn't?"

"I've got no idea," Lauren said honestly. Because she didn't want to worry Ginny, she added, "It was probably just a routine inquiry. Still, I can't figure out why no one's identified him by now."

"Does seem kind of strange, him being so—"

"I know, so good-looking."

"Well, you got to admit, he would tend to stick in somebody's mind, now wouldn't he?"

That was certainly true in her case, Lauren thought, but she wasn't about to admit it. Instead, she chatted a few minutes longer with Ginny, then went to the locker room to change.

By the time her duty shift started, she was already helping to stabilize a young man who had gotten himself stabbed in the course of a disagreement with members of another social organization, namely a gang fight. She didn't get another chance to think about "her" John Doe until several hours later when she finally took a brief break.

She was heading into the nurses' lounge, intending to get a cup of coffee, just as Litzer was getting off the elevator. He saw her and called out.

"Hey, Walters, got a minute?"

For the top neurologist at St. Mary's, she supposed she did, but the thought of that coffee made it tough.

"What's up?" she asked.

"I wanted to talk with you about our friend, Mr. Doe. You know they moved him to post-op?"

"No, I didn't, but I figured it would be soon. How's he doing?"

"Physically, better than any man has a right to expect. His recuperative powers are amazing. Mentally's another story."

"Still no memory?"

"Zippo. Which brings me to why I'm here. I kind of got the impression that the two of you hit it off pretty good."

"What gave you that idea?" Lauren asked.

"Just that he asked about you, wanted to know if you were on ER again." Litzer gave her a little grin. "Far be it from me to read into anything, but I wondered if maybe you could try to find a little extra time to drop by and talk with him. Having someone around he feels comfortable with might help."

"I don't know—"

"I really mean it. So far he's textbook, but if he doesn't start remembering soon, there are gonna be problems. What happens if we get to the point where we're ready to release him and he still has no idea who he is? You think we should just turn him over to social services?"

Lauren hadn't thought of that. It horrified her. "There's got to be some alternative—"

"Not unless he starts regaining his memory. Think about it, until he remembers who he is, he has no access to money, much less food or a place to live. He'll have to go into a shelter."

"That's ridiculous. This is obviously a man who was doing very well for himself. He comes across as intelligent and educated, and his clothing indicates a high-level income. There has to be some alternative—"

Litzer shrugged. "I can try to get him a bed in an after-care facility, but you know how scarce they are. It's tough enough to get a fully insured patient in, much less an indigent."

"He is not indigent."

"He might as well be. Without his identity, he effectively doesn't exist. We'll do the best we can, but it won't be pretty."

Lauren shook her head in disgust. "I can't believe this. You're telling me that a patient with amnesia is just going to be released onto the streets where he'll have to depend on social services to keep him from being homeless?"

"I don't like it any more than you do. I'm just telling you how it's going to end up. Better he remembers who he is, and soon."

"I'll see what I can do," Lauren said. She was appalled by what Litzer said, but she couldn't argue with him. He was a good doctor—and a caring person. He just didn't fool himself about how the world worked.

John Doe had managed to survive a shooting that would have finished most people. But he was very far from being out of trouble.

Lauren's shift ended six hours later. She saw Martha coming down the hall and ducked into a stairwell to avoid her. Feeling guilty—but determined—she climbed the steps to the second floor post-op ward.

John was in a large room to the left of the nursing station. There was room for four beds. One was occupied by an elderly man who was asleep. The other two were empty for the moment.

Lauren approached cautiously, unsure whether he would be awake or would want to see her, notwithstanding what Litzer claimed. He was awake, though, and staring out the window. When she cleared her throat, he turned and looked at her.

A quick smile flashed across his face. "Hi, there. So you found the place."

She didn't let him see her relief, but it was there all the same. Sitting down in the chair beside the bed, she said, "I'm a little surprised to find you on your own."

"So am I. Let's just say the service here is a whole lot more attentive than I would have expected."

"I'll bet," Lauren said dryly. She was willing to put money on every nurse, aide, candy striper and a high proportion of the female doctors finding some reason to wander by, if they hadn't already.

"So how are you doing, really?"

He shrugged. "I hurt, but I expect to. I feel a lot stronger and the food actually tastes good to me, so I figure I'm getting better."

"What about your memory?" Lauren asked gently.

"That doctor, Litzer, suggested I talk to one of the staff psychiatrists. He thinks there might be techniques I could use to joggle things back into place."

"What kind of techniques?"

"Relaxation, visualization, stuff like that."

"It doesn't sound as though you think they'll work."

"I don't know," John admitted. "I'm getting fragments, split seconds of images that don't make any sense. It's as though the memories I should have somehow got turned into a kind of jigsaw puzzle and all the pieces were tossed up in the air."

"And, of course, there's no picture on the box to help put them back together."

"Exactly. Litzer still says he thinks everything will come back of its own accord, but I get the impression he's starting to worry."

Lauren hesitated. Choosing her words with utmost care, she said, "Is there a chance that you may not want to remember something."

He shot her a hard, penetrating look. "Such as?"

"I have no idea, but you went through a terrible experience. It's not impossible that some part of you simply doesn't want to remember."

"I don't like the idea," he admitted, "but I suppose there could be something to it. That's why Litzer wants me to talk to a shrink?"

"There are a lot of reasons for talking to a psychiatrist," Lauren hedged. "But yes, that might be one of them."

"I'll have to think about it. In the meantime, I know what would make me feel a whole lot better real fast." The smile he gave her was nothing short of provocative, a combination of cajolery and seduction.

"What would that be?" Lauren asked. She suspected her pulse had just shot up, but so what? Lots of stuff could cause that.

"A shower," he said, "and a shave. Think you could arrange it?"

"Possibly." That was not a twinge of disappointment she felt, not at all. "We'll need to put a plastic covering over the bandages."

"And some real clothes?" he added.

"Some people want everything. First, let's find out if you can stand."

He could, although he was a little shaky to start with and had to lean on her. Quickly enough, he regained his balance.

"There are safety bars in the shower," Lauren told him when the plastic was in place. "Make sure you use them. The last thing you need right now is a bad fall."

"Yes, ma'am."

"I'll see what I can do about pajamas," she said as he disappeared into the bathroom. A moment later, she heard the shower running, followed by whistling.

When she returned ten minutes later, the water was still on. Lauren knocked on the bathroom door.

"I'm putting pj's in here for you," she called.

"Thanks, how about a razor?"

"I've got that, too, but you're supposed to sit down to shave. Okay?"

He grumbled, but didn't really object. A few minutes later, the shower was turned off, and shortly after that he emerged.

At least, she presumed it was him. Same height, same midnight hair, same silver-gray eyes, same build. Oh, yes, definitely same build, but this was not the ailing patient who had almost died short days before. While he still had something of the pallor of illness, not to mention the bandages wrapped around his torso, he stood upright with an air of vigor and strength that was striking. The pajamas she'd found fit him well enough, but they did nothing to conceal the breadth of his shoulders or the grace of his long, muscular limbs.

"Litzer's right," Lauren murmured. "Your recuperative powers really are amazing."

"Let's just say I'm highly motivated. Now about that shave—"

"You'll have to get back into bed first."

He made a face but didn't object, leading Lauren to believe that he wasn't quite as strong as he wanted to think. Once he was lying down, she slid a hospital table into position in front of him and popped open the top to reveal a mirror. With that, a basin of hot water, a tube of shaving soap and the razor, he was all set.

"I never thought a shave could feel this good," John said as he began removing several days' worth of accumulated beard.

Or look that good, either, Lauren thought. What was it about a man shaving that was so intrinsically appealing? The simple masculinity of the act had never really struck her before, but it sure did now. She had to make an effort not to stare. Especially once she got a glimpse of what the razor was revealing.

Okay, so he was square jawed, his mouth chiseled with a purity a Greek sculptor would have envied. Was she really surprised? Obviously, nature had been in one of its overendowment modes when his particular genetic blueprint was put together.

"Finally," he said as he ran a hand over smooth skin. "I can't remember going this long without a shave before except one time—"

He broke off, his eyes darkening.

"One time what?" Lauren asked softly.

"One time when I was on a fishing trip with some buddies. We were off in the mountains someplace, camping out for days. It was great. I remember the smell of wood fires and flipping trout in a cast-iron skillet."

"That's great."

He met her eyes, his own filled with relief. "Maybe Litzer's right. It will all just come back."

"Sounds like it's already started to. Do you have any idea who the friends you were with might be?"

"Not really. Just an idea there was one called Bull and another...Jamie...Jimmy...something like that."

Nothing followed, though he clearly tried. After a few moments, he shook his head in disgust. "I can see that clearing in the woods, the stream, everything, but I can't make out anyone's face or remember a full name."

"Give it a little more time," Lauren advised. She emptied the basin into the sink, then rinsed and dried it. "Right now, I think you should rest."

"I've been doing enough of that. What I need is to get reconnected with the real world."

"Want me to turn on the TV?"

"God, no, most of what's on is drivel."

"See, something else you just found out about yourself. How about some books or magazines?"

"That would be great, if it's no trouble."

"It isn't. Any preferences?"

He thought for a moment. "Mysteries, I think, and anything with news."

"Oh, one other thing," she said as she was about to leave. "You might want to know that there have been two phone calls inquiring about you. One was from a man who identified himself as a reporter for the *Trib*. The other caller didn't leave a name."

"Or give mine?"

Lauren nodded. "Afraid not. The guy who said he was from the *Trib* was told your condition had been upgraded to stable, nothing else."

"What about the other one?"

"He wasn't given any information."

"Who do you think he was?"

Lauren shrugged. "I can't say since I didn't speak to him myself, but I'd guess just some curiosity seeker."

"Surely people have something better to do than call up a hospital about a patient they don't even know?"

"You'd be amazed at the things that happen around here. Anyway, if he calls again—or anyone else does— I'll make sure you're notified."

He nodded. "I'd also appreciate it if no information was given out."

Lauren assured him that wouldn't be a problem. As was the case with every other patient, he had a right to privacy and confidentiality.

"I'll bring that reading material as soon as I can," she said, but she wasn't sure he heard her. He was staring off into space. If the hard glitter of his eyes was any indication, his thoughts were far from pleasant.

Chapter 5

When John heard Lauren's footsteps recede down the hall, he reached for the phone. It took a call to information and several false starts before he got through to the number he wanted.

"Impoundment," a bored voice said.

His hand tightened on the phone. "I'm calling about a car."

"Yeah, so?"

"A BMW, picked up Monday night on the upper East Side. Is it there?"

"Gotta have the license number."

"You know, it's the damnedest thing. I never bothered to memorize it."

The civil servant on the other end made a sound of disgust. "Color?"

John hesitated. He would have to guess. If he was wrong, any chance he had of finding the car was over.

"Black." It felt right. Beyond that, he couldn't be sure.

"Hold on."

He was left in phone limbo. Minutes passed, three...four. He thought maybe he'd been forgotten but finally the receiver was picked up again on the other end.

"Yeah, we got it. You want it back, come down here and bring a hundred twenty-five bucks."

John assured him that he would. Quickly, he added, "Just so you won't have to go to the trouble when I get there, what's the license number?"

The man read it off grudgingly. John wrote the numbers down fast. He was tempted to ask whether it was a New York plate, but that was sure to tip the guy off that something was wrong. He would just have to find out for himself when he got the car back.

And he would get it back. All he had to do was get out of the hospital. Oh, yes, and find a hundred and twenty-five dollars. Piece of cake.

He swung his legs over the side of the bed and stood. It hurt, but not as much as it had earlier. Besides, the pain was good. It reminded him that he was alive.

His gaze fell on the bedside table. The card the detective had left was there. Why didn't he just call the guy, tell him what he'd found out about the car and let him do the rest. There was a good chance that they would have an ID on him before nightfall. At the very least, he would have access to money.

That he didn't reach for the phone again told him clearly which way his own thinking was going. Like it or not, he could no longer deny that his memory was starting to come back. And what he was remembering wasn't good. Not by a long shot.

He remembered a room, men sitting around a table on which the remnants of a meal remained. Ruby red wine gleamed in long-stemmed crystal goblets. Candles flickered, illuminating fine china and silver on a damask cloth. Much of the room was in shadows, but it looked luxuriously furnished, with fine artwork on the walls. High windows opened onto a terrace. Guards moved back and forth across it, keeping watch.

There was an air of contentment and general well-being. The men were in an excellent mood. They were all business associates and their business was doing very well indeed.

He was one of them, sitting there at that table, drinking the wine, enjoying the success. One of them in the shadow world they inhabited, a world of immense wealth and power that reached all the way from the hidden coca plantations of Latin America to the streets of every American city, town and suburb.

His stomach clenched. He was swept by a wave of disgust so intense that he wanted to lash out and hit something. With the greatest difficulty, he controlled himself, but only just.

To the very core of his being, he prayed he was wrong. But the vision of ruby wine sparkling in candlelight kept returning to torment him. He stood at the window, staring out at the city, and tried to convince himself that he was not what he so feared he might be.

Lauren had managed to put together the reading material John wanted without any difficulty, but she didn't get a chance to take it up to him. The ER suddenly had one of those runs it got from time to time with a bus accident, two probable heart attacks, a rape and a shooting all coming in on top of one another.

In the rush that followed, she managed to convince an orderly to take the books and magazines upstairs. After that, there was no time to think about John or anything else except the work at hand.

It was quitting time before she was able to draw a free breath. Thinking she could use a cup of coffee before going home, Lauren headed for the nurses' lounge. As she went past the nursing desk, Ginny called to her.

"Got a minute? There's a couple of guys here who want to talk to you."

Two men in dark suits were standing at the desk. They were clean shaven, their hair neatly trimmed. Both looked about thirty. The taller one smiled slightly.

"You're Ms. Walters?"

"That's right. What can I do for you?"

"Is there somewhere we can speak privately?"

Lauren hesitated. She caught Ginny's curious look and returned it, making clear that she had no idea what this was about. "Privacy's kind of at a premium around here," she said. "Would you mind identifying yourselves?"

"Sorry, of course. I'm Agent Becker and this is Agent Hollis. FBI."

Both men reached into the breast pockets of their jackets and withdrew small leather folders. Flipped open, they revealed badges that were indeed stamped

FBI and accompanied by what appeared to be identification cards with the FBI seal.

"I see..." Lauren said quietly. "Are you sure it's me you want to talk with?"

"You were the senior nurse on duty when the John Doe shooting victim was brought in Monday night. Is that correct?"

"Yes, it is, but there were also a doctor and resident, not to mention the whole trauma team."

"And we'll be speaking with them, too," Agent Becker said soothingly. "But Ms. Germaine here mentioned that you were better acquainted with him."

Ginny shot her an apologetic look. "I didn't really say that. I just mentioned that you'd been spending a little extra time—"

"It's all right," Lauren said. After all, it wasn't as though Ginny had said anything that wasn't true.

"Are you going off duty now?" Agent Hollis asked. He was slightly shorter than the other man and a few pounds heavier, but they both had the same smoothly professional air.

"Yes, I was—"

"Then perhaps we could just walk out with you. That would be all right, wouldn't it, Ms. Walters?"

"I suppose—"

Lauren wasn't sure exactly how it happened, but before she could take a breath she was walking toward the ER doors with an agent on either side of her. The one called Becker had a hand lightly touching her right arm.

"Is this really necessary?" she asked as they stepped outside.

"It won't take long. We just want to ask you a few questions."

But they were walking her toward a dark car parked halfway down the block. Two men were in the front seat, watching them approach. They looked considerably rougher than Becker and Hollis, with longer, unkempt hair and dressed in leather jackets. Were they undercover agents? Why were they here with the other two?

Why were they taking her to the car?

"I forgot something inside," Lauren said. "I'll just be a minute—" She would go back to the ER, call security and have the men checked out more carefully. She'd never seen an FBI badge in her life, except on television. Belatedly, she realized that she had no way of knowing if theirs were authentic.

"It can wait," Hollis said. "Just answer our questions first."

They were within ten yards of the car. The man in the passenger side seat was getting out to open the back door.

Lauren dug in her heels, trying to stop, only to find herself propelled along by Becker and Hollis. Each man had hold of her now. They were almost at the car.

"Stop!" Her voice rang out, filled with the fear she genuinely felt.

A few heads turned as people on the street glanced in her direction.

"Let me go!" Lauren shouted. She wrenched away from the two men, taking them by surprise. In the moment it took them to realize what was happening, she ran.

People stared, but no one made a move to help. She didn't expect it. All she could think of was to reach St. Mary's. She would be safe there.

She could hear the men behind her, cursing. A hand brushed her sleeve. For an instant, she was caught. With a desperate sob, she pulled free and threw herself through the doors of the emergency room.

"Lauren—"

Ginny's eyes were wide with shock. She came around the desk quickly and put an arm around Lauren. "Honey, what's the matter?"

Lauren looked back over her shoulder. She could see Becker and Hollis on the other side of the doors. The looks on their faces were terrifying, but they made no effort to come inside.

She tried to speak, couldn't get her breath, then tried again. "Those men—"

Ginny steered her over to a chair. She sat her down and crouched beside her so that they were on eye level. The older nurse was a friend, but she was also an extremely capable professional. Quietly, she said, "Everything's okay now. No one's going to hurt you. Now you just take your time and tell me what's wrong."

Lauren shook her head. "No time. Call security. I don't think those men are FBI agents."

Ginny stared at her for a moment. Abruptly, she stood. "Stay there, I'll be right back." She hurried over to the desk.

Lauren didn't wait. She jumped up and ran for the elevator. The doors were just closing. With a groan, she turned to the stairs. She had to reach John and warn him.

He was awake and mercifully alone.

"You have to get up," she said, grabbing for the robe at the foot of the bed. "C'mon. Ginny's calling security by now, but we have to move you, at least for a little while."

He stared at her for a split second, taking in her flushed and disheveled appearance and the fear in her eyes. Calmly, as though nothing at all unusual were happening, he got up, took the robe and in the same motion started leading her out of the room.

"What's going on?" he asked matter-of-factly when they reached the hall.

"Two men came," she began, marveling at how unruffled he was. "They said they were from the FBI, but I don't think they are. They tried to get me to go with them into a car. They said they wanted to talk about you, but I got scared and ran."

"I see," he said. His hand was on her arm. Without seeming to do so, he was steering her toward the stairwell. "What did they look like?"

She described Becker and Hollis briefly, as well as the other two men who had been waiting in the car. "I was thinking we'd go to the lounge. They won't look there—"

"They'll look everywhere they can," he said as reasonably as though they were discussing the weather. "I need some clothes."

"Clothes? No, I didn't mean you should leave the hospital. You can't. It's too soon yet. I only—"

"Clothes," he said again. They were in the stairwell, heading down toward the first floor. "There must be a men's locker room. Where is it?"

"There's one behind the ER, but—"

"Let's go."

Lauren went only because she had no choice. Getting him out of his room had been her idea. She'd only thought to protect him until the men could be identified. The idea of leaving the hospital was crazy. He would see that. Any minute now, he would realize that he should just wait while security handled the matter.

"I can't go in there," she objected when she opened the door to the men's locker room.

"Yeah, you can. This will only take a minute."

The locker room was mercifully empty. Faster than she would have believed possible, he went down the row of lockers until he found one that hadn't been securely closed. Lauren suspected it was Felix's. He'd complained more than once that he had a habit of doing that. Inside were a pair of khaki trousers, a flannel shirt and cowboy boots.

"You can't just take those—"

"I'll return them, I promise," he said as he pulled the clothes on. "Let's go."

"Go where? Whoever those men are, security will deal with them. You can't go—"

They were back outside the locker room in the small hallway that ran between it and the ER. Lauren glanced through the glass panel of a door and saw a security guard hurry by.

"Over here!"

She meant only to convince John that there was no reason to leave. If he saw the security guards, realized that they existed and were there to protect him, surely he would understand he was in no real danger.

The guard heard her and pushed open the door. He was a young man, in his mid-twenties, well built but not especially muscular. His expression was puzzled. He glanced at John, then turned his attention to Lauren. "Something wrong, miss?"

Lauren never got a chance to reply. Before she could draw a breath, John moved. He launched himself straight at the guard, hurtling him against the wall. In an instant, he had the man's gun in his hand and a choke hold around his throat.

"Don't do anything stupid," he said. Glancing around, he spied a nearby utility closet. Gesturing with the gun, he said to Lauren, "Get his keys."

"My God, what are you doing—?"

"Do as I say. Get his keys."

Numbly, Lauren obeyed. She felt as though she had stepped into a nightmare.

"See if he's got one for the locker room," John said.

"He won't. It's never locked. People have to be able to come and go at all hours."

"What about that?" He cocked his head toward a nearby office, one of several small consultation rooms that were used occasionally but not often.

One of the keys on the guard's ring fit the lock for it. John shoved the man inside, took the keys and fastened the door securely. There was no telephone in the room. Until someone heard the man shouting, which he was already doing, he would be stuck.

"Come on," John said. He slipped the gun into his pants pocket but kept his hand on it. The look he gave Lauren suggested she would be smart not to forget that it was there.

"Why are you doing this?" Her voice was little more than a whisper.

A fleeting look of regret passed across his face. "There's no time to discuss it," he said. "Let's go."

Chapter 6

Lauren had never jumped a subway turnstile before in her life, but she did so now. Part of her prayed they would be caught. The other part worried about what would happen if they were. Visions of the gun made her stomach tighten. She kept silent and went along, hoping against hope that John would realize what he was doing was wrong and relent.

They caught the train going downtown and got off five stops later. John kept a hand to Lauren's back as they made their way through the station and up to the street.

It was midafternoon. People were coming and going at the usual frantic pace. No one took any notice of them.

"Where are we going?" she asked finally as they headed west in the direction of the Hudson River.

"To get my car."

"Your car? You remember where you left it?" If he did, what else did he remember? Enough to make him run?

John shook his head. "I didn't remember, I just got lucky. I figured it might have been towed and it was."

The impoundment lot sprawled across a dozen acres of what had been old docks along the river. It was surrounded by a fence topped by razor wire. A large building housed the clearing office.

As they stepped inside, John stopped and looked at her. Very softly, he said, "It would be a serious mistake to try anything here."

"What do you think I'm going to do? Scream my head off and give you an excuse to start shooting?" All the bitterness she felt at his betrayal of her trust—and her own foolhardiness in trusting in the first place—spilled out in those words. She felt perilously close to crying.

His eyes darkened. "I have no intention of hurting anyone, least of all you. Just behave yourself."

Without even checking to see if she followed, he headed for the desk.

Lauren was only a few feet from the door. She could have been out it and away in seconds. The temptation to do exactly that swept over her, but it died almost as quickly as it arose.

She couldn't leave him. He was still recovering from the wounds he'd suffered. There might be any number of explanations for his bizarre actions. He could have a head injury they knew nothing about. He could be reacting to the mix of drugs he'd been given. If she walked away from him now, she would feel unbearably irresponsible.

And beyond all that, in some private place she didn't particularly want to examine, was the undeniable fact that she had come to care too much about him. He was no longer simply a patient.

Slowly, she followed him to the counter.

"A hundred and twenty-five bucks," the man on the other side was saying. "Ain't nothing I can do without that. Also, I gotta have your license and registration."

"It's all in the car," John said.

The man looked doubtful. "Your license, your money, you left that stuff in the car?"

John shrugged, looking apologetic. "'Fraid so. Look, I know you've got a lot to do. What do you say we just grab the keys and walk out there. I'll pay you on the spot."

"I don't know."

"I hate to put you to any more trouble. Say, you don't mind hundreds do you? That's all I've got."

"Oh, great, now you're telling me I have to bring change?"

"No," John said, "I'm not telling you that."

The man stared at him for a long moment. Finally, he shrugged. "Whatever you say. Lemme see—oh, yeah, number 468. Okay, let's go."

They walked out onto the lot. Lauren could barely breathe. She was terrified of what would happen when they got to the car. What if John was making all that up about the license and the money? She didn't even have her purse with her. Ignoring for the moment the total impropriety of helping him, she couldn't pay for the car even if she wanted to.

Number 468 was a sleek black BMW. "Nice," the man murmured. "You got the keys?"

John nodded. He put a key in the lock. Lauren had the fleeting impression that he was holding his breath, but the key turned and the lock sprang open. The relief that flashed across his face was intense, but he masked it quickly.

Opening the glove compartment, he reached inside. This time, he couldn't hide his reaction. He was clearly surprised.

The man didn't notice. He glanced at the registration John held out to him and nodded. "What about the money?"

From the thick roll of bills he held, John peeled off two. He handed them over. "That takes care of it, right?"

"Yeah, right. You're all set. Give this to the guy at the gate." He presented John with a stamped form attesting to his right to remove the vehicle and slid the bills into his pocket.

"You remembered about the money?" Lauren asked when they were both in the car.

John turned the key in the ignition and shook his head. "Not really, but I guess I must have had some idea that it was there."

"He never asked for your license." His license would have had his name on it, but surely the registration did, too?

"Good thing since I still don't have it. The car's registered to something called Pilgrim Consolidated in Boston, whatever the hell that is."

"They'll be looking for you, you know," Lauren said when they had left the lot. "I'm sure the security guard has been found by now."

"You think taking the guy's gun is going to make the cops want to talk with me again?"

"Yes."

He actually laughed. "Sounds like a safe bet. That's why I don't plan on hanging around." He turned the car south toward the Lincoln Tunnel, which connected Manhattan with New Jersey. Once across, it was possible to go anywhere.

"What do you plan on doing?" Lauren asked. She was rather proud of how calm she sounded, especially when she felt anything but.

"I plan on figuring out who I am. I'd like to be able to do that without any interference from either the police or the guys who showed up at the hospital. By the way, did they hurt you?"

He asked it almost casually, but there was a steely edge to his tone that startled Lauren. Considering that he himself had threatened her with a gun and virtually kidnapped her, his concern seemed misplaced.

"No," she said curtly. "They didn't."

"You're sure?"

In fact, her arm ached where Becker had gripped it, but she didn't think this was the time to mention that. "All they did was scare me so much that I ran back to try to help you. Chalk that up to one of the stupider things I've done in my life."

"Actually, it was especially stupid since you have no idea who I am. Didn't you think at all about what you might be getting into?"

"No," Lauren admitted. She folded her arms across her chest and stared out the window. She felt scared, embarrassed and disbelieving all at once. Her life had been so orderly up until now. Even working in an occupation that seemed to breed chaos, she'd prided herself on never acting impulsively or carelessly. Obviously, she'd been saving that all up for one big blowout and, boy, was it a doozy.

"So you're going to go off and try to get your memory back," she said. "Is that it?"

"I don't see what else I can do. Hanging around the hospital waiting for the Bobbsey Twins to show up doesn't seem too smart."

"What about the fact that you still need medical attention?"

"I'm fine."

"No, you're not."

"Yes, I am."

This was certainly an intelligent discussion they were having. Lauren decided to end it.

"You're bleeding."

John glanced down at himself, startled. They were just entering the tunnel. Its bright yellow lights illuminated the slow spread of blood across his shirt. He muttered an obscenity, but didn't slow down.

"Important safety tip," Lauren said. "After being shot twice in the chest and once in the stomach, it is not a good idea, repeat not, to jump out of bed, go running through the hospital, wrestle a security guard and hightail it for parts unknown. Extensive medical research into this subject supports the idea, however silly it may sound, that bed rest is actually the better alternative.''

John grunted, an eminently masculine sound of dismissal. ''You're a sarcastic little thing, aren't you?''

''I am not a little thing. As for the sarcasm, call it honesty. If we don't get that bleeding stopped quickly, you're going to be in serious trouble.''

''Like I'm not now?''

''Okay, more serious trouble. When we get out of the tunnel, look around for a drugstore.''

He grumbled, but a few minutes later, when they had reached the New Jersey side, John pulled into the parking lot of a large mall. ''There's got to be one here.''

''Stay in the car,'' Lauren said.

He shot her a quick, hard look.

''If you get out, somebody's going to notice the blood on your shirt. Do you really want to have to answer questions about that?''

''No,'' he said quietly.

''I need some money. In the rush, I seem to have forgotten my purse.''

He reached into his pocket, removed the wad of bills and peeled off several.

Lauren opened the car door. ''I'll be back soon.''

He nodded, but she had the distinct impression that he didn't quite believe her.

Alone in the car, John leaned his head back and closed his eyes. He was exhausted and hurt like hell, but that was the least of it. Was he totally insane to have done what he had? Breaking out of the hospital like that, stealing a gun, getting Lauren to come with him? Getting? His mouth tightened. Call it what it was. He'd kidnapped her.

That was the downside. The upside was that if what he feared he was remembering about himself were true, all he'd done was add to what was undoubtedly a long criminal record.

The shooting, the BMW, the memory of that dinner with the men around the table, the wad of money in the glove compartment, even the skill with which he'd disarmed the guard, his own familiarity with guns, the easy way he'd bribed the guy at the impoundment lot— all suggested that he was someone he simply didn't like very much.

Okay, he hated. The thought of what he seemed to have done with his life disgusted him. He was filled with self-loathing. For a fleeting moment, he seriously thought that it would have been better if Lauren and her pals at St. Mary's hadn't been quite so good at their jobs.

But they had been. He was alive, and it was up to him to make the most of it. But how? What exactly was he going to do besides try to stay alive. And keep Lauren in the same condition.

She hadn't thought of that, he was sure. It hadn't occurred to her that she was in real danger. There was no guarantee that Becker and Hollis—and whoever had sent them—would back off her just because he'd disappeared. On the contrary, they might go after her all the more, figuring she was the link to him.

And he'd let her get out of the car and disappear. Great, really great. She had money, she had guts and she surely had enough sense to hightail it away from him as fast as she possibly could. Straight back to St. Mary's and whatever danger awaited her there.

He cursed under his breath. Why hadn't he stopped her? So what if he was bleeding? He could handle that. It was Lauren he cared about. If she was hurt—

Pain twisted through him. He put a hand to the damp spot spreading over his shirt and clenched his teeth hard, trying not to groan.

Lauren found a drugstore on the first floor of the mall. She quickly bought what she needed. Her intention was to go straight back to John, but as she was leaving, she spotted a men's clothing store. On impulse, she dashed inside and managed to locate a shirt she was reasonably sure would fit him. Anything else would have to wait.

On her way out of the mall, she passed an electronics store. The front display windows were filled with television sets. Out of the corner of her eye, she glimpsed what looked like the front entrance to St. Mary's. A reporter was standing there, holding a microphone. She couldn't hear what he was saying, but it wasn't hard to guess.

Without waiting to see more, she started across the parking lot. She was within sight of the BMW when she saw John getting out. Or at least trying to. He staggered slightly and had to lean against the car for support.

"What are you doing?" she demanded as she caught hold of him. "Are you out of your mind? Get back in the car."

He gave her a slightly dazed smile. "You're here."

"Of course, I'm here. Where did you think I'd be?" The look in his eyes said it all. "Never mind. Switch over to the passenger side. I'm driving."

That he did so without protest told her more than anything else about his condition. Masking her own fear, Lauren slipped behind the wheel and quickly maneuvered the car out of the parking lot.

"We have to find someplace secluded where I can change your bandages."

He turned his head against the seat rest and looked at her. "We?"

Lauren didn't take her eyes off the road. Only the tightening of her hands on the wheel revealed the emotions warring inside her. She had crossed over a crucial line from innocent victim to accomplice—and they both knew it.

"Like it or not," she said, "I'm still a nurse and you're still bleeding. I think you should return to New York and turn yourself over to the authorities, but I don't really believe you're prepared to do that. So either I walk away and let you possibly bleed to death, or I do what I was trained to do and keep you alive."

"Was it a hard choice?" John asked laconically.

"No," Lauren admitted. Then she said nothing more, preferring to concentrate on finding somewhere safe from prying eyes.

They were on an empty stretch of road that ran alongside the interstate. There was an underpass up ahead, Lauren noticed. Old tires and bottles lay tossed among the uncut grass. The place looked virtually abandoned.

"Here," Lauren said and pulled the car into the area of deepest shadow. With the medical supplies she'd bought, she got out of the car and opened the passenger door.

John was very pale. His features were tightly drawn and his breathing was more rapid than normal.

"How much pain are you in?" she asked as she began to unbutton his bloody shirt.

"Some."

"Come on, the truth."

"Okay, a lot, but I don't want any drugs."

"That's good, since the strongest thing I can buy is over-the-counter." She got the shirt open and eased it off him carefully. The bleeding was bad, but not quite as much as she'd feared.

Going as slowly as she dared under the circumstances, she cut away the old bandages and examined the wounds. "Considering what you've been up to, this could be a lot worse."

"That's nice to hear."

"Yeah, well, try this. You've ripped out a few stitches, not many but enough to start the bleeding again. I'm going to have to resuture you. It's going to hurt."

There must have been something in the tone of her voice. He touched a hand lightly to her hair. "It's okay, Lauren. Just do what you have to."

Somehow, his willingness to comfort her made the whole thing worse. Lauren prayed for calm. She'd done thousands of suturings over the years. This one wasn't even particularly difficult. Except, of course, for the fact that they were in a car instead of a hospital and she had no anesthetic and only the most primitive antiseptic. Except for that, everything was great.

John took a deep breath and relaxed back against the seat. Lauren was startled to see how the tension went out of him, as though merely through an act of will he was placing himself in a calm, almost meditative state.

Wishing she could do the same for herself, she set to work.

Chapter 7

It was over, thank God. She'd gotten the bleeding stopped, the new bandages on; he was even wearing the clean shirt. Now they were heading north.

It would be dark in a few hours. John was asleep in the passenger seat, but she suspected it was more of a light doze. What he needed was good solid rest, preferably under medical observation, antibiotics and maybe more steroids to speed healing. What he had gotten was a nonprescription pain pill that probably had barely dented what he was feeling and a fast ride to an unknown destination.

The city was a good hundred miles behind them, but Lauren had no feeling of safety. She was sure that state troopers in the entire tri-state area would have been warned to look out for them. Would they know about the black BMW, perhaps even have its license plate number? Maybe not. Even if the man at the impoundment lot saw the news and put two and two together, he might be reluctant to call the police. Explaining how he'd let the car go could be tough.

So perhaps their luck would hold and they would make it to wherever it was they were going. What then? She knew he was hoping his memory would return, but with each passing day there was less chance of that. Somehow, she had to make him understand that he couldn't go it alone. He needed help.

But he wasn't the kind of man who would accept that easily. Although he had seemed genuinely grateful when she repaired his wounds—and this despite the pain she knew she was inflicting—she also sensed that he wasn't used to depending on anyone.

Or at least she thought she sensed that. When it came down to it, she had nothing but her instincts to guide her. What if they were wrong? What if she was falling prey to his physical attraction and the raw aura of masculine power she felt from him?

She'd heard of such things happening. There was the so-called Stockholm Effect, for instance, the tendency of captives to identify with their captors, feel sympathy for them and even see them as basically good people. But she was a trained professional with, if anything, more than her fair share of common sense. Surely she could trust her own judgment?

In the final analysis, she had little choice. With a sigh, she returned her full concentration to the road.

Another thirty or so miles slipped away before Lauren realized that she needed to stop. She considered trying to find a private spot off the road, but then decided that something a little more formal would be better. Besides, she was also thirsty and hungry. John probably didn't feel like eating, but he had to have liquids or his condition would worsen.

When she spotted the next Food and Gas sign, she turned off the main highway. Arrows led her to a small shopping center with a service station and a grocery. John awoke just as she was pulling up to the pump.

"Where are we?" he asked, sitting up.

"Getting gas. It's self-serve. I'll go pay and find out where the rest rooms are."

When the tank was full, Lauren pulled the car into a spot to the side of the grocery store. "We need food and drinks. Is there anything you prefer?"

"Just make it cold."

She returned a few minutes later with two large bags of bottled water, soda and the most nutritious snacks she could find. Unlocking the door to the trunk, she started to put the bags in only to stop abruptly when she saw what was already there.

"John—" she called. "I think you should see this."

He got out and walked over to where she stood. A low, hard expletive broke from him. Together, they stared into the trunk.

That was an M-16 assault rifle, he had no trouble at all recognizing it. Next to it was a 9 millimeter Smith & Wesson not very different from the one that had shot him, except it didn't have a silencer. Several boxes of ammunition were neatly stacked next to the weapons. There was also a small black bag.

"Let's get away from here," John said quietly. He took the bag out of the trunk, slammed the lid down and returned to the front of the car. Lauren followed.

She was silent as they drove away from the shopping center. Nearby was an office building that had emptied out for the evening. They parked behind it.

John unzipped the black bag. His hand shook slightly as he opened it, but otherwise he betrayed no emotion.

"The missing wallet," he said as he took it out of the bag.

It was dark brown leather and looked as expensive as everything else he'd had with him. Flipping it open, he withdrew the driver's license.

"John Santos," he read quietly. "What do you know."

Lauren leaned over so that she could see the picture. "That's you."

"Sure seems to be. Says here I live in Vermont, I don't have to wear glasses and I want to be an organ donor. Somebody could have gotten lucky the other night."

"Stop it," Lauren said. She was appalled enough by the situation without him making morbid jokes. "This is definitely not the way an amnesia victim is supposed to rediscover his identity, but at least you can put a name to yourself now, and you know where you live. Does any of that help?"

"Sure it does. I didn't particularly like the name Doe, and I wasn't looking forward to being homeless."

At the look on her face, he sighed apologetically. "I'd suggest you give me a good, swift kick except you just might do it. Look, I'm sorry about all of this. There's no way you should be in this situation, but you are and I'm concerned those bozos who showed up at the hospital won't just let it drop."

Lauren started to speak, but he forestalled her. "They know you spent time with me and they've got to be wondering how much I told you. The fact that I can't remember anything won't impress them. If they can't get to me, they'll come after you."

"The police—"

He shook his head. "I want to know what I'm dealing with before I walk into any police precinct."

"You realize that even knowing your name now, you simply may not remember on your own?"

"I know that's possible, but I think my memory is starting to return. I'm getting fragments of things more and more. None of it's pulled together yet, but I believe it will."

He turned and looked at her. The dim light reflected off the hard planes and angles of his face. "I want you to go somewhere safe. I'd suggest family only if they live outside New York, but it might be too easy to trace you there."

"I really wouldn't want to involve them, anyway," Lauren said.

"What about friends?"

"Sure, except they're in New York and I wouldn't want to involve them, either. Besides, you're overlooking something. Actually, several things."

"Like what?"

Lauren hesitated. What she was about to do was flatout nuts. He was offering her the perfect chance to walk away—better yet, run. Maybe work really had been getting to her and she was having some kind of breakdown. Certainly her normal rational self seemed to have disappeared.

"You need help," she said. "I know you hate to admit it, but that's how it is. I was as careful as I could be, but your wounds could become infected, or open again."

"That's my problem, not yours."

"Okay, how about this, then? You say those guys are likely to come after me and I'm inclined to agree. So where exactly am I supposed to hide? Without any credit cards or identification, I can't check into a hotel or rent an apartment. I won't involve my family or friends, so what do you suggest I do? Go back to the hospital and get my purse? Wouldn't that be a little like walking into the lion's den?"

"I understand your point, but—"

"There are no buts. If I get out of this car, I have nowhere to go."

"What about the police? You could sure as hell go to them."

"Oh, that's a great idea. They would love to hear my story, all about how you made me go with you at gunpoint, but then I hung around to help, bought bandages for you and so on. I'm sure the people at the mall would be only too happy to tell them that no one was holding a gun on me then, not to mention the guy at the service station and in the grocery store. I could wind up in jail. You do realize that, don't you?"

He gave her a wry look. "Actually, I was hoping *you* wouldn't."

"Well, I have, and no thanks. I'd rather take my chances with you."

Quietly, he asked, "Do you realize what you're saying?"

"Only too clearly. We're stuck with each other until you figure out what's happening and why."

She sounded a whole lot braver than she felt, but that didn't matter. What she said was true. They had to live with it.

"I'm really sorry," he said gently.

Would a big-time criminal apologize like that? Lauren didn't think so, but then she was hardly in a position to judge.

"I've got one question," she said.

"What's that?"

"How do we get to Vermont?"

The usual way, apparently. John seemed to remember the route well, as though he had driven it often back and forth to New York. It was still a long trip. The dashboard clock was close to midnight when they finally found the dirt road outside the small town that he believed was the right place.

"Are you sure?" Lauren asked, peering into the darkness. She had the headlights on high, but they didn't help much. The night was moonless with thick cloud cover, stygian.

"As sure as I am about anything. Besides, we're in Appleton."

That was the town listed on his license, more than a wide spot in the road, but, for a city girl like Lauren, still the back of beyond. And so incredibly dark—

"I can't see," she said.

"You're doing fine. It's not that bad a road."

"According to you."

The road was dirt, narrow and winding. It led up what seemed to be the side of a mountain, but which Lauren knew was probably nothing more than a good-sized hill by Vermont standards.

At the end of it, when they finally got there, was a cabin. An honest to goodness log cabin nestled in a grove of pine trees with a small porch out in front and a fieldstone chimney rising above the roof.

John got out of the car slowly. By the glow of the headlights, he stared at the cabin. "I remembered this."

"Did you really?"

He nodded. "I saw an image, a vision. I don't know what it meant, but it was day and there was smoke coming from the chimney."

"Is it home?"

"Yes, I think it is."

"What about New York?"

"Nothing comes to me. Let's see if we can find a way in."

The key was hanging from a nail behind one of the window shutters. It only took twenty minutes or so to locate.

"So much for my memory returning," John groused. "I can't even remember where I left the key."

"Have you got any idea why you weren't carrying it?" Lauren asked. "Or for that matter, why your wallet was in that bag?"

He turned the key in the lock and stood aside to let her enter first. "None at all." With the flick of a light switch, which he located unerringly, the interior was illuminated.

The outside of the cabin was decidedly rustic, but the inside was entirely different. Lauren's breath caught as she took it in. It didn't exactly look as though it came straight out of a fashion magazine, it was too personalized for that, but the effect wasn't completely dissimilar.

The downstairs was one large room centered around a fieldstone fireplace. Comfortable couches and what looked like an authentic Persian rug were scattered in front of it. To either side were built-in bookshelves that looked completely filled. Framed Early American portraits hung on the walls along with folk-art wood carvings. A pine table and chairs were between the seating area and a compact but well-equipped kitchen.

The only slightly incongruous note was a worktable set against one wall, equipped with a computer, printer, phone and fax machine.

"This is wonderful," Lauren said. Actually, she thought it looked like something out of a dream, the sort of place she could fantasize about but had never really expected to be in. What a marvelous world it was that such a haven could exist mere hours away from the city and all the turmoil of St. Mary's.

John looked around, taking in the room as though he were seeing it for the first time.

"Do you recognize things?" Lauren asked.

"I'm not sure. It just feels right. I'm glad to be here, not to mention relieved." He frowned slightly. "It doesn't seem to really tie in with the BMW and the fancy clothes, though, does it?"

"Maybe you like to get away to something really different, a change of pace."

"Maybe," he said, but he looked unconvinced. "Let's see what's upstairs."

They climbed the stairs to a loft set back into the eaves of the roof and extending out about half the length of the main floor. Most of it was taken up by a large sleeping area furnished with another Persian carpet and a king-size bed covered by a star-patterned quilt in varying shades of blue. Tables on either side of the bed were piled high with books. Beyond the sleeping area, a door stood open to reveal what looked like an unusually large and well-equipped bathroom.

John opened the doors to a double closet. He whistled softly. "Seems I'm not exactly an all-work-and-no-play type."

Lauren peered over his shoulder. Half the closet was taken up by an assortment of sports and business clothes, all in keeping with the general tone of affluence. But the other half was crammed full with sports equipment, everything from tennis and squash rackets to skis, scuba gear, a basketball, climbing ropes, even a set of oars.

"I just thought of something," Lauren said. She turned toward the steps.

John followed. Downstairs, tucked away to one side of the stairs, were a small group of framed photographs. Several showed a group of men crewing one of the low, sleek sculls used for rowing.

"That's you, isn't it?" Lauren asked, pointing to one of the men.

John looked more closely. He nodded. "Sure seems to be." He studied the photos. "There's something on the team shirts, but I can't make it out. Wherever these were taken, they appear to be more than a few years old."

Lauren had to agree. The man standing beside her was definitely older than the man in the picture, perhaps by a good ten years or even slightly more.

"They're probably college pictures," she said. "If we can get a magnifying glass and see what's on the shirts—"

"We could figure out where I went to school."

She nodded, excited. "Alumni associations tend to keep good records. We might be able to learn where you work and—" She froze, suddenly realizing what else they might discover.

"And whether I'm married?" John asked quietly. "I've thought about that and I'm convinced I'm not. Besides, there's no evidence of a woman here."

That was true. The cabin was purely a masculine domain.

"Maybe you have a wife who doesn't like the country," Lauren suggested. Her voice was very low. She wanted desperately not to care, but couldn't manage it.

"I don't think I'd marry someone like that," John said. "But you've got a point. We should try to follow up with whatever school this was. Let's keep an eye out for a magnifier."

He glanced at the photos again, then held up his hands so that he could see the palms. "I wonder if I still row. That would explain these calluses."

"We're on a lake," Lauren said. "If you do row, there's bound to be a boat around here. Let's take a look when it's light."

Abruptly, she shivered. The excitement of reaching the cabin and discovering what it held was beginning to wear off just enough for her to realize how chilled she was. The temperature seemed to be falling fast and she only had on her hospital gear.

"You'd better put on warmer clothes," John said. He reached into the closet and removed a flannel shirt, a sweater and a pair of khakis. "Meanwhile, I'll get a fire started and see if there's any other heating system."

Hugging the clothes to herself, Lauren watched him go back downstairs.

Chapter 8

There was a small basement under the house. John found it with little difficulty and was relieved to discover what looked like a relatively new furnace and hot-water heater. Both started without difficulty, which suggested they'd been used in the not-too-distant past.

Back upstairs, he checked to be sure the fireplace flue was open, then using tinder and wood stacked nearby, quickly got a good-sized blaze started. His chest hurt a little, but not as much as it probably could have, given what he'd been doing.

When the fire was going, he sat back and looked around the room. It was definitely familiar. He had the feeling that the place was important to him and that he came there as often as he could, but he didn't live there all the time. Much of his life was elsewhere. The cabin was more of a sanctuary, a place to escape to.

But from what? The men seated around the table?

The man he feared he might be?

He passed a hand over his face wearily. None of it was going to get solved tonight. Besides, he had Lauren to think of. And to protect.

He still could hardly believe that she'd come with him—or that he'd let her. But she did have a point. Where could she go without any identification? Even with all the money he could give her—he figured he had several thousand dollars in that roll—she wouldn't get far. So long as she refused to involve family or friends, and he couldn't blame her for that, she had nowhere else to go.

Which made her his responsibility. He'd endangered her unknowingly, but that didn't change anything. The more he thought about it, the more convinced he was that he'd been right to get her away from St. Mary's and from New York. There was no way Becker and Hollis were FBI. Real federal agents didn't go around forcing women into automobiles. There was a protocol, a procedure.

They would have used one of those private consultation rooms to question her. It would all have been very low-key, very quiet. She would have been asked at least twice if she wanted an attorney present. The entire conversation would have been recorded.

Hell, after some of the lawsuits that had come down in recent years, he wouldn't have been surprised if they'd asked her permission to videotape the interview.

Which begged the question, how exactly did he know all that? Had he himself been on the receiving end of the FBI's attention, at least enough to know how such things went?

The soft sound of footsteps coming down the stairs broke his train of thought. He let it go gladly. Sooner rather than later, he would have to deal with the harsh possibilities of who he was. But for now he was glad to be able to think of other things.

First and foremost among them, Lauren. She had put on the warmer clothes he'd given her, and it looked as though she'd also washed her face and tried to comb her hair, apparently with her fingers. In the process, the cool, competent professional he was used to seeing had vanished, replaced by a young and rather vulnerable woman of fey beauty and bewitching grace.

"I hope you don't mind," she said softly, "I borrowed a tie from the closet to use as a belt. The clothes—" she held out her arms and smiled "—are a little big."

In fact, she swam in them, like a child playing at dress-up. Except it was no child who crossed the room toward him and looked worriedly into his face.

"How are you feeling?"

"Fine," he said. His voice sounded unnaturally husky. He cleared his throat and tried again. "I've got the heat going—and the fire. How about something to eat?"

"That would be great. Do you think there's any food?"

"I haven't looked yet, but I'm pretty sure there's something."

"Let me," she said. "Unless you really want another sample of my needlework, I suggest you sit down."

John sat. Much as he hated to admit it, he had almost no strength left. That, and the fact that having stitches done without anesthetic hurt like hell, made him decide to let Lauren have her way. Not that he intended to make a habit of it. Not at all.

He would just rest for a few minutes. There was no harm in that. After all, it had been an eventful day. A man had a right to a little rest.

He awoke sometime later to the sound of plates being set on the table. As he started to get up, Lauren smiled apologetically. "Sorry, I was trying to be as quiet as I could. But supper is ready. You should try to eat."

Still groggy, he came over to the table. She'd found soup and the fixings for sandwiches. He sat down slowly, staring at the food.

"The soup was canned," Lauren said as she took the chair across from him. "So was the tuna. You keep a pretty full pantry, by the way. There's a little hall leading to a back porch. It's got a full-sized freezer in it. That's where the bread came from. By the way, the refrigerator was still on, but it was empty. Either you hadn't been here in a while, or you weren't expecting to be back for some time."

Which was it? John wondered. He tried to picture himself moving around the cabin, doing ordinary domestic things like cleaning out the refrigerator. What had he been thinking of, planning?

"Did you notice anything else?"

She nodded. "I don't know much about wine, but I'll bet you do. At least, there's a large rack filled with bottles next to the freezer."

"Doesn't sound like I came up here looking for a simpler way of life."

"Oh, I don't know. After all, you can't remember how you lived anywhere else." She put down her sandwich and looked at him. "Can you?"

"If you mean can I remember a place where I think I lived besides this one, no, I can't."

"What about anything else—faces, names, any idea of what you might do for a living, presuming, that is, that you actually work. Maybe you inherited money."

"I don't think so. At least, that doesn't feel like me." He let it go at that and turned his attention to the soup, which, though canned, was quite good. Or maybe he was just unusually hungry. He'd been living on hospital food for the past couple of days and before that, IVs. Besides, he was glad of an excuse not to answer her. The vision of those men, their sleek faces and pleased expressions, troubled him deeply. He wanted to believe that he was this man—of the cabin and the sports equipment, with fondness for good wine but peaceful living. But if he was, where had the money come from to support such a way of life? What exactly had he done to earn it?

And what explained the guns in the back of the car, the wallet hidden away, or all the rest?

"I think I've had enough," he said a few minutes later. "I'll give the fire a poke."

"Thanks. We should probably get some rest soon. I'll take the couch."

"It'll be warmer upstairs. Heat rises."

"That's okay," she insisted. "I'll be fine here."

He went over and tossed another log on the fire. Fatigue weighed down on him. Food, warmth and a relative sense of safety were combining to make him realize how desperately he needed to sleep.

"Take the bed," he said as he picked up his dishes. "I don't feel right, you sleeping on the couch."

"That's ridiculous. This is your place and, besides, you're the one who was hurt. The couch is fine." She joined him, carrying plates and bowls to the sink. "Go on. I'll clear up."

"That's not fair."

Lauren stopped in midstep and stared at him. "What?"

"It's not fair. You cooked. I should clean up."

Her eyes widened. "Where did you get that from?"

"Get what?"

"Fair. Woman cooks, man clears. Who gave you that idea?"

He could see what she was thinking. Either he had a mother who deserved every woman's gratitude, or he had a wife who demanded equal treatment. Which was it?

"My mother, I think," he said, and managed a smile. "She had five boys. If she hadn't raised us right, she would have gone nuts."

Lauren set the dish down that she'd been holding and stared at him. "Did you just remember that?"

"Yes . . . I did. There were five of us, all sons. In . . . Brooklyn, I think."

"You don't have a Brooklyn accent, not even a New York one, for that matter."

"Whatta ya mean, New Yoick accent? New Yoickers don' have no accent. Everybody else has an accent."

Lauren laughed, but she turned serious quickly. "I think your memory really is coming back."

"I sure as hell hope so." He put the last of the dishes in the sink and ran water over them. "Let's be wild and finish this tomorrow. I'm going to make up the couch."

"Thanks, but I can do that. Why don't you go upstairs?"

He turned the tap off, dried his hands and put them on his lean hips. From the decidedly unfair advantage of his greater height, he stared down at her. "I'm not going upstairs because I'm sleeping on the couch. If you want to join me there fine, but it's going to be a tight fit."

Lauren blushed. The color washing over her cheeks struck him as fascinating. Amnesia or not, he couldn't remember the last time he'd seen a woman blush. If pressed, he would have said they didn't do that anymore. But he would have been wrong, at least where this one woman was concerned.

"You're incredibly stubborn," she said.

"I'm stubborn? Look who's talking."

It got very quiet suddenly. He could hear the wind blowing outside the cabin and tree branches rustling. A log popped on the fire.

"All right," Lauren said. "I'll take the bed. Good night."

Softly, to her back, he replied, "Good night."

* * *

She lay in his bed and stared up at the rough-hewn wood of the ceiling. The roof of the cabin sloped, so that if she reached up she could brush her fingers along the planks.

It was comfortably warm in the loft. The air was fragrant with the smell of the fire. She had bathed quickly, then put the flannel shirt back on. As big as it was, it made a more than adequate nightgown.

Snuggled down in the bed, under the star-patterned quilt, she felt her eyes grow heavy. Jumbled scenes from the long, tumultuous day drifted through her mind.

Had so much really happened in such short amount of time? The men coming to the hospital, her sudden fear, John's actions, the ride to Vermont? All that?

It was well after midnight. She should have been in her apartment, getting enough rest to go back on duty in the morning. Instead, she was here, on the run from the authorities with a man she barely knew and who still hardly knew himself.

Five sons…Brooklyn. Guns in the trunk of the car. A secluded cabin that spoke of money and taste. A need for privacy. Books, lots of books. About what? She should find out in the morning. It might be a further clue. Try to get the name of the school he rowed for…call— Lauren slept, more deeply and dreamlessly than she had in months.

And awoke to screams.

She was out of bed in an instant, responding on pure instinct. Still groggy, hardly aware of where she was, Lauren raced down the steps in the direction of the screams. By the time she reached the main room, she was alert enough to know it was John calling out. She flipped the lights on and rushed to the couch.

He lay twisted in the covers, his face bathed with sweat, his eyes open but unseeing. One arm lashed out, almost catching her in the midsection.

"No, damn it! Robbie! Nooo!"

He sat up, then started to rise. The covers fell back. She realized with a start that he was sleeping naked.

"Robbie!"

Without thinking, Lauren threw her arms around him. She was far more worried that he was going to hurt himself than her. If he tore the stitches open again...

His skin was hot to the touch. Was it fever or just the terror that had him in its grip? With no way to know, she held on as tight as she could and spoke soothingly.

"John, it's all right. You're in the cabin in Vermont. It's all right."

For a horrible moment she thought he couldn't hear her. His grip hardened on her arms. She bit back a cry of pain and put both her hands on his face, cupping his jaw and forcing him to look at her.

"It's me. Lauren. Please wake up, John! Please!"

He blinked once, twice, and then, like a man awakening from a trance, realized who she was. Instantly, his hold on her loosened.

"Lauren...I'm sorry...what happened—?"

She took a deep breath, fighting for calm. "You were having a nightmare, I think. You cried out." As she spoke, she gently eased him back onto the couch and drew the blanket over him. "I'm afraid you may have a fever. Do the wounds hurt more than before?"

He shook his head slowly. "No, I'm fine. That dream—" He stared off into the distance, still dazed.

"I'll be right back. I want to get cold compresses."

When she returned moments later, he was still lost in thought. Gently, she wrapped a couple of wet towels around his wrists and put another on his forehead. He shivered slightly as the cold water touched him, but otherwise didn't react.

Lauren sat down beside him. She put two fingers to his wrist and surreptitiously checked his pulse. It was still a little rapid, but strong and slowing quickly.

Somewhat relieved, she waited silently, giving him time to come to terms with what had happened.

"Did I say anything?" he asked after a short time.

"You mentioned someone named Robbie. You seemed very worried about him."

Pain flitted across his face. "He was my brother, one of them, anyway."

"Was?"

"He was killed in a stabbing." John swallowed with some difficulty. "At least, I think he was. Maybe my mind's just inventing this stuff."

"I doubt it," Lauren said quietly, thinking of her own tendency to tell herself important, if painful, facts in dreams. She removed the compress and felt his forehead again. His skin was already much cooler. What she'd feared might be fever seemed to be disappearing.

"This is usually how memory returns after severe trauma," she said. "It comes in fragments loaded with emotion. I'm afraid if you're dreaming of a brother being stabbed to death, it probably happened."

"I was there. I could see it, but I couldn't do anything." He leaned forward and put his head in his hands. "It was as though I was paralyzed."

"Is it possible that it happened recently and that it's at least partly responsible for your memory loss?"

"I don't know—he looked so damn young. I think it was years ago."

He lifted his head. Their eyes met. His glittered, silver against the diamond droplets of unshed tears. "Do you have brothers or sisters?"

"Both, but all thankfully alive."

The fire had died to embers. Lauren stood and went to put another log on it. When she came back to the couch, John reached out and took her hand.

Silently, he drew her to him. The fire leapt. His chest was very dark against the blanket. She watched the steady rise and fall of his breathing and tried not to think.

When his hand cupped the back of her head, she made no protest. They had been coming to this through all the long day, coming to this place and this moment, to this truth.

His mouth was gentle, patient, asking more than demanding. A deep shudder coursed through her. She felt his skin, unshaven, rough against hers, smelled the scents of wool and soap, of maleness, knew a surging need so alien to herself, yet so familiar.

Caution, so tightly held for so long, slipped as though from between her fingers and flew away into the windswept night.

Chapter 9

Sunlight streaming in through the windows on either side of the fireplace woke John. He sat up slowly, rubbing a hand over his chin, and looked around.

The cabin seemed empty. There was no sign of Lauren.

With the blanket wrapped around his waist, he went into the kitchen. There was a pot of coffee on the counter and a note.

"Gone for a walk. Back soon. L."

Reading it, he frowned. He wanted her there, with him, close enough to touch and talk to, to smell the honey fragrance of her hair and see the quicksilver flash of her smile.

That was ridiculous. She had a perfect right to go for a walk.

Back soon. He would be smarter to do what he needed to before she returned.

With a mug of coffee in hand, he went upstairs and turned on the shower. While it heated, he found clothes in the closet and set out shaving equipment. When the water was ready, he stood under it, head back, eyes closed and let it wash over him. His bandages were getting soaked, but he didn't care. He'd already decided to change them himself when he was done. He'd been depending on Lauren long enough.

In the midst of rubbing soap over his chest, he paused. The mere thought of her was enough to send a wave of desire through him so intense as to be almost painful. He bit back a groan and shook his head ruefully. Fragmented though his memory was, he had the definite impression that he was generally more in control when it came to women.

Not with this one, though. Not by a long shot.

He turned off the water and began drying himself. The khakis he'd laid out were lightly starched and had a crisp crease down the front. He put them on, then studied the bandages.

Wet as they were, they couldn't be too hard to get off. The tape was already peeling at the corners. He gave a small tug, felt it clear through to his spine and sighed.

There was only one way to do this. With a single rip that left him gasping, he got the bandages off and, for the first time, looked at himself.

His first thought was that it could have been a whole lot worse. There were three dark lines of sutures running across his chest, two near his left lung, one further down in the stomach area. The skin around them looked red, but there was no sign of infection. He touched himself gingerly and was pleased to discover that the pain had lessened considerably.

Using the supplies Lauren had bought, he fashioned a fresh bandage that, while somewhat more ragged than the one she'd done, was still serviceable. That done, he set about shaving.

When he was clean shaven and fully dressed, he went back downstairs. There was still no sign of Lauren. The day looked bright and clear. He told himself she would be fine on her own.

First things first, though. He needed to bring in the guns from the trunk of the car. Trying to decide where to put them, he opened a small closet near the front door. It contained a rain jacket, a pair of boots and a gun rack.

The rack was large enough for six good-sized weapons. It already held two—a Kalashnikov assault rifle and an older self-loading carbine. On the floor behind the rack were neatly stacked boxes of ammunition. A box on the shelf above held a Heckler & Koch handgun with room left over for the pistol that was still in the car.

John took a step back and studied the contents of the closet. These were serious weapons, not the kind a casual, weekend hunter might have around. So why were they there?

What, exactly, had made John Santos believe that he needed them?

For an instant he saw again the image of his brother falling, blood gushing from his side. As objectively as he could, he forced himself to consider what he knew. His memory said that Robbie, his brother, had been stabbed and was going to die. Nothing could change it. But it had all happened years ago. He was more sure of that than ever.

Why, then, did he feel there was a connection between the loss of his brother and the guns in the closet?

His head had begun to throb. Ignoring it, he went out to the car, popped the trunk and took out the guns. He had just finished putting them away in the closet when Lauren returned.

She came up the road slowly, a sheaf of wildflowers in one hand. Her head was down; she looked lost in thought.

She also looked incredibly beautiful, fresh and desirable, so much so that he felt again the same savage thrust of hunger he'd experienced earlier. Her short, softly curling auburn hair gleamed in the sunlight. She'd put on the same clothes she'd worn the previous night. Not even they could conceal the slender grace of her body.

When she looked up suddenly and saw him, his breath caught. For an instant, it was as though her mouth moved against his as it had the night before, soft, pliant, infinitely sweet.

She stopped, visibly gathering herself, and forced a smile that did not reach her eyes. Those, he saw, remained cautious.

"Good morning," she said.

He nodded politely, not taking his gaze from her. They might have been two strangers, meeting at a country crossroads.

"Beautiful day," he said.

She nodded politely. "I went for a walk."

"I found your note."

"Oh, good, I didn't want you to worry." She came toward him slowly, her smile more real now. "How are you feeling?"

"Fine. I changed the bandages."

She faltered. "Did you?"

"Somebody's going to invent an adhesive that doesn't hurt to take off and make a fortune."

"Oh, someone already did, but we in the medical community decided to suppress it." She shot him a look of mock sternness. "Wouldn't do to have patients think they could rip off their bandages whenever they liked."

"I'm not a patient anymore," he reminded her, gently but with no mistaking his meaning.

She averted her eyes and stepped inside the cabin. "I found a boat."

He shut the closet door, glad that she hadn't seen what was inside. "Did you really?"

Lauren nodded. "There's a shed near the lake. It's in there."

"How big a boat?"

"Small, like the one in the pictures, but not as long."

"A one-man scull. Did you find anything else?"

"No, of course I'm not sure what I'm looking for, either. This place is incredibly beautiful, but there doesn't seem to be another house anywhere nearby. Also, there's no sign of anyone having been around here recently. No tire marks or traces of campers."

"The land's posted." He knew that suddenly, without having to think about it. There were no other houses because he owned all the land, several hundred acres. It was posted to prevent hunters or others from wandering onto it.

He valued his privacy.

She nodded once, accepting that yet more of his memory was returning, then went into the kitchen. As she passed him, their bodies brushed.

Instantly, she moved away, but not quickly enough to prevent him from reaching out. His hand caught hers.

"Lauren—"

"Please—"

"About last night—" He stopped, unsure of what to say. That he was sorry? He was, but not for the kiss they had shared. Sorry that it hadn't gone much further, that they hadn't spent the night entwined, that he hadn't woken up with her still in his arms.

Somehow he didn't think that was what she wanted to hear.

"We were both tired," she said and gently disengaged her hand. "How about breakfast?"

Turning away before he could answer, she began getting out plates.

He set the table. She rummaged through the freezer, finding orange juice, bacon and English muffins. The silence drew out between them until finally John said, "I'd like to really go through this place. Search it from top to bottom and find everything there is to find that could help me remember."

"That sounds like a good idea."

"Care to help?"

"I'd be glad to, but I don't want to intrude."

Unspoken between them was the knowledge that some of what was found might not be pleasant.

"I'd still appreciate it," John said. Somewhere between putting the guns away and spreading marmalade on an English muffin, he had decided that it was better for them both to know it all. As much as the truth could hurt, at least there would be no misunderstandings.

Lauren nodded. "All right. Where do you want to start?"

He took the bedroom, beginning with the closet. Lauren stayed downstairs. She began with the bookcases, examining each volume and checking to make sure nothing was hidden behind them.

He seemed to enjoy a wide range of reading. She found everything from histories and biographies to mysteries and science fiction. There was even a well-thumbed copy of Daphne duMaurier's *Rebecca*. But there were no hidden documents, nothing to explain who John Santos was.

"Any luck?" he asked just as she was finishing.

"Not really. How about you?"

"I dress well, and I seem to enjoy a lot of different sports. Also, I'm very neat. Other than that, nothing."

"Nothing? Not a letter, not a receipt? Absolutely nothing?"

"Zero. I even checked the medicine cabinet for prescriptions, figuring they'd have a doctor's name on them, but there aren't any."

"I haven't done any better here," Lauren said. "You like to read and you have a broad range of interests.

Oh, there is one thing. I'd say you're more interested in words, and possibly in writing, than most people."

"What makes you think that?"

Lauren pointed to a two-volume set of books in a slipcase. "You've got the compact edition of the *Oxford English Dictionary,* possibly the most complete guide to the language ever put together."

John bent down and looked at the set. There was a small drawer in the top of the slipcase. He opened it carefully.

"A magnifying glass," Lauren said. "I should have thought of that. The type in this set is so small there's no other way to read it."

"Let's see how good it is with those photos."

He took several from the wall and spread them out on the pine table. Holding the magnifying glass, he studied the shirts the oarsmen were wearing.

"It's hard to make out—"

Lauren bent closer. "Let me take a look."

She squinted through the glass, struggling to read what looked like words wrapped around an ornate symbol.

"Dei sub numine vigit." Yikes, how long was it since she'd struggled through Latin, trying to learn enough to make sense of all the medical terminology? "Under God she . . . grows?"

"Prospers," John said. "It's the motto of Princeton University."

"You went there?"

"I don't know—"

Lauren gestured to the phone on the worktable. "Let's call them and ask."

They tried, only to be reminded that it was Saturday morning. The administration office was closed and wouldn't reopen until Monday.

"It was still a good idea," John said. "I'll call back, but in the meantime—" He looked around the cabin. "Short of taking the walls down, there aren't too many more places to look."

"There's that," Lauren said, and nodded her head at the computer.

Chapter 10

"Damn it ! I've tried everything."

Lauren lowered the book she'd been reading. It was a history of the Crusades and really very interesting, enough so that she had only glanced up perhaps fifty times to look at him. Fortunately, he hadn't noticed.

His mouth was set in a hard line of impatience. She remembered how it had felt against her own and suppressed a shiver. A lifetime of caution had come very close to being forgotten the previous night.

Such behavior was so uncharacteristic that she could still hardly credit it. A stranger seemed to have awakened inside her, a woman of sensuality and languor for whom conscience was but a distant murmur. A woman she wanted desperately to ignore.

Work on the computer wasn't going too well, she noticed. John looked tired, frustrated and generally fed up.

"How about Rumpelstiltskin?" she suggested.

"Tried it."

"You're kidding. You really did?"

"About an hour ago, along with Goldilocks, Cinderella, Pinnochio, Peter Pan and Santa Claus. I've tried every password I could think of. Nothing works."

"Maybe it's something really obvious like your middle name. What is it by the way?"

He ran a hand through his thick ebony hair and looked away. "I don't see any reason to get into that."

She straightened up, interested now. "Why not? It could be that, couldn't it?"

"No, it couldn't."

A smile started to creep across her face. "Oh, Lord, how bad is it?"

"Bad."

"I only got a peek at your license. What does it say?"

He hesitated. Finally, with a palpable note of disgust, he said, "I'm having real second thoughts about my parents. What kind of people would name a helpless infant John Wilbur?"

"Wilbur? Really, your middle name is Wilbur?"

"Would I say it was if it wasn't?"

"No," Lauren admitted. She debated for a moment, then said, "It could be worse."

"Tell me how."

"It could be Chastity."

He laughed. "Nobody would name—" Abruptly, he broke off and stared at her. "Lauren *Chastity* Walters?"

"No, actually it's Chastity Lauren Walters. I just don't use my first name for rather obvious reasons."

His gaze swept over her in a purely male assessment, touched, lingered, flicked away all in an instant. For the merest flash, she looked into the silver eyes of the wolf, cunning, intelligent, not incapable of gentleness. Then it was gone, carefully masked, or perhaps it had been merely her own illusion.

"I suppose you were treated to all the jokes that sort of thing would provoke?" he asked.

"Every one of them, so don't tell me about names. Have you tried Wilbur?"

"Two hours ago."

She sighed. They were getting nowhere fast, but since they seemed to have nowhere else to go, maybe it was worth spending a little more time trying to crack the computer.

"How about Appleton?" she suggested.

"Tried it. Also Vermont, mountain, skiing, maple syrup, slalom, snow, you name it."

"Scull. Did you try that?"

He nodded. "Along with rowing, oars, oarsman, crew, crewing and Princeton. Oh, yes, also tiger."

"Why tiger?"

"It's the Princeton mascot."

"You remembered that," she said, trying to find something encouraging.

"Along with all the stanzas to 'Old Nassau,' but I don't see how that's going to help."

She stood and came to stand beside him. He was sitting slumped in a chair, staring at the computer. It was open to a Windows start-up screen, but beyond that he couldn't access.

"It's probably safe to say you're not a hacker," Lauren observed.

"Fair bet. You'd think I would have written the password down somewhere in case I forgot it."

"There's hardly a scrap of paper in this place apart from the books. It looks as though you kept everything on the computer."

"Good for me. Too bad I can't access any of it."

He stood, gave the screen one final look of disgust and switched it off. "I'd like to get out for a while. How about showing me that boat you found?"

Lauren agreed quickly. Now that he was no longer so distracted by the computer, she was glad for an excuse to leave the cabin. Beautiful though it was, it made her feel too close to him, too confined. Too liable to say—and do—things she would later regret.

"It's getting colder," she said as they walked outside. John locked the door behind them. He did it automatically, then pocketed the key. Even here, in this pristine seclusion, he seemed driven to take precautions.

She didn't comment, but merely added that observation to her growing store of impressions and, truth be told, concerns. There was so much about him that she couldn't reconcile. When she thought of the books and the guns, the serenity of the place he had made for himself and the horror of being shot down on a city street, it seemed as though he were almost two different men leading separate and distinct lives.

The man she was with now appeared content to stroll to the lake along a path strewn with pine needles, hands thrust into his pants pockets, and survey the glory of the landscape all around them.

To the north and west, the land rose in a spectacular ridge of mountains, part of the Green Mountains chain. Spring had not yet settled in as firmly as it had in New York. Melting patches of snow could still be seen down low on the mountains. The air had a snap to it and there was a hint of wetness, as though the snow might not be completely done yet.

They followed the path as it twined through the pine forest to the edge of a glacier-carved lake. Except for the chirping of a few birds and the distant rush of water, the silence was absolute. They might have been the only people on earth.

The lake lay to the east of the cabin. A long, wide finger heading south almost as far as she could see. A cloud of mist seemed to rise off the lake at the far distance of her vision.

"What is that?" she asked.

John looked in the same direction. "Falls. If you listen closely, you can hear them."

That was the rush of water she had noticed, the lake tumbling in a torrent that sounded almost like the far-off roar of a locomotive.

"How high are they?"

"At least a hundred feet. It's a spectacular sight. We could hike down there if you like."

She sighed but restrained herself. There was probably no point in mentioning that it wouldn't occur to most people who had been shot just a few days before to hike several miles along rugged terrain in order to view waterfalls.

"I'd just as soon not do it today," she said, and let it go at that. "The shed's over here."

It was a small, well-built structure, and looked as though it could stand up to all sorts of weather. There was a single-paned window built into the door. John looked inside.

"That's what it is, all right."

"Any idea where the key might be?"

"No, but if I run true to form, it's probably right around here somewhere."

It wasn't. Despite their best efforts, the key couldn't be found. They had to content themselves peering in through the single pane of glass on the door. There was little to see beyond the scull itself, oarlocks and some old canvas. Like the cabin itself, the shed was tidy, well-organized and minimally revealing.

When they were done, they stood, staring out over the lake. Lauren remained silent. She had never been one of those people who felt compelled to talk all the time. Perhaps it was the stress of her occupation, but periods of intense quiet had always struck her as one of the greatest luxuries life had to offer.

At least fifteen minutes passed before John spoke. Quietly, not looking at her, he said, "I think it's time I leveled with you."

Lauren raised her head, startled. Her own thoughts had been drifting in that comfortable, unordered way that happened all too rarely. Now she suddenly felt wrenched back into a harsher reality.

"What do you mean, level?"

"There are things I've remembered that I haven't told you about."

"Such as?" Exactly how much had he kept from her? Had his memory returned entirely? Even as that possibility arose, she dismissed it. Perhaps she was being the world's greatest fool, but her instinct was to trust him.

"This is very difficult," John said. He sat down on a rock beside the lake. Lauren joined him. She tucked her arms around herself, only partly because she was chilly.

"Why don't you just take it step by step?" she suggested.

He shot her a grateful look. "You're very understanding."

"It goes with the job."

"Is that what this is?" He shook his head as though reprimanding himself. "Never mind. Look, we both know that there are things about me that don't jibe with my being Mr. Nice Guy. The guns in the trunk of the car, for instance. What I did to that guard, not to mention forcing you to go with me."

"Then there's the getting shot part."

"Yeah, that, too. Anyway, back at the hospital, I got this flash, a memory of sitting around a table in a very luxurious house, having dinner with a group of men. I was one of them, part of what was going on. We were there to talk business, which apparently was going very well."

"So? Lots of people discuss business over dinner."

"With armed guards walking back and forth right outside?"

"I see. What kind of business do you think you were there to discuss?"

"Drugs," he said flatly. "I've considered other possibilities—guns, mainly. But I really think it's drugs."

"You think you're a drug dealer?" Her eyes were wide and dark. It wasn't as though she hadn't thought of it herself, the Colombian coin in his pocket added to everything else had made her wonder. But for him to come right out and say it—

Reluctantly, he nodded. "I think there's a strong possibility."

"You're jumping to conclusions. There are a lot of other things that suggest you're nothing of the sort."

"Such as?"

"This cabin for one. What self-respecting drug dealer would choose to live in the backwoods of Vermont? And then there's your choice of reading material. You deal drugs when you're not perusing the *Oxford English Dictionary* or any of those hundreds of other books you've got? Plus, you went to Princeton, for heaven's sake. That's not exactly my idea of a breeding ground for crime."

"There're people who went to the Ivy League and turned out to be bad guys. Okay, maybe they were mainly into white-collar crime, but that doesn't mean I couldn't have gone further."

"What are you, then, an overachiever? Oh, I don't think embezzling or inside trading is enough for me, I think I'll get into drug dealing? Come on, that just doesn't add up."

He laughed faintly. "I'll admit it sounds a little strange put that way."

"No, it sounds a lot strange. For all you know, you were having dinner with the president of the United States and the armed guards were Secret Service agents."

"Do they do that?" he asked, amused. "March up and down, holding guns?"

"How would I know? I'm not the one who got invited to the White House. I just think you should give yourself the benefit of the doubt."

"Okay, then how do you explain Becker and Hollis? If they're real FBI agents—which I don't happen to believe—why are they curious about me? And if they're not, then what am I into that would involve me with people like that?"

"People like what? Rude? Clumsy? Presumptuous?"

"Wait a minute. They tried to force you into a car. You were scared to death."

"So maybe I let my imagination run away with me. Maybe you're doing the same thing."

He sighed and looked at her with such gentleness that her throat tightened. "You're a kind woman, Chastity Lauren Walters. Not to mention a beautiful one."

She was having a little trouble breathing. Nothing serious. Any second now, she would be fine. "Don't call me that."

John smiled. He reached out a hand and stroked the back of it along her cheek. "Why not? What's wrong with Chastity?"

His smile deepened, daring her to answer. She would have, too, except she was suddenly awash in confusion. That other woman, the familiar stranger, was stirring again, making her presence unmistakably known.

"I think we should go back," she said and noted distantly that she didn't sound anything like herself at all.

By the time they reached the cabin, the temperature had dropped noticeably. With the sun slanting westward, long shadows fell across the clearing. A mist of frost was already appearing on the windshield of the BMW.

It was warmer inside, but when John said he would get a fire going, Lauren was glad. She went upstairs to take a shower, needing time to herself and a chance to get her thoughts in order.

It didn't work. When she came back down forty-five minutes later, she was scrubbed clean and her hair shone with tiny droplets of water still clinging to it. She had put on the same pants but a clean shirt. It hung down almost to her knees.

Music was playing on the stereo. Vivaldi, Lauren thought. John was back in front of the computer.

"Any luck?" she asked.

"None. I'm down to trying titles from the bookcases."

"Is it possible the password isn't in English?"

"Anything's possible." He stood slowly and stretched.

She watched, unwillingly fascinated. His body was so long and lean, so superbly fit. Whatever he did, he didn't spend a great deal of time behind a desk.

"I'll fix dinner," she said and turned away quickly.

Chapter 11

"Gin," Lauren said. She spread her cards out on the table and smiled. "Read 'em and weep."

John shook his head in disgust. He dropped his own hand. Lauren began adding them up.

"A cardsharp," he said. "I should have known."

"It's pure skill."

"Pure bull would be more like it. Let's play again."

"You've already lost five hands."

"My luck's got to turn."

Though they played for another half hour, Lauren continued to win. Finally, John gave up. "Let's play something I'm good at."

Her eyes widened slightly. "Isn't that a line from an old Steve McQueen movie?"

He nodded. "The *Thomas Crown Affair*, except they were playing chess."

Lauren remembered. She also recalled what the Steve McQueen character thought he was good at.

"Poker," she said quickly. "I'll bet you're a lot better at that."

He sat back and surveyed her. "How much?"

"How much what?"

"How much will you bet?"

"I didn't actually mean that. It's just a figure of speech."

His smile was a blatant challenge. "What's the matter, losing faith in all that pure skill?"

"No—"

"I'll tell you what. Forget poker, we'll play gin again. If you win, you get to name the prize. If I win, so do I."

"Wait a minute, I'd be crazy to agree to that since I have no idea what you'd want."

Actually, she could think of a few things, but she wasn't about to admit that.

His expression turned serious. Looking her straight in the eye, he said, "If I ask for something you don't want to give, you can just say no."

"Isn't that welching?"

"Not in this game."

Interesting rules. Lauren didn't think she'd ever encountered them before. But then there was a first time for everything.

"All right," she said slowly. "You deal."

He did with, she thought, a bit more agility than he had shown before. The look he shot her as he examined his hand was not reassuring.

Gin rummy had a lot of associations for Lauren. She'd played it as a kid with her brothers and sisters, and at school with her friends. There had been long nights pulling extra duty when an occasional round of cards helped pass the time. She'd even played it once in the back of an ambulance while waiting to collect bodies from a plane crash, something she still felt guilty about even though she knew it had been prompted by the need to escape the anguish and horror even highly trained professionals felt in such a situation.

Sometimes she won, sometimes she lost. She'd never really cared all that much either way. For one thing, there was never much at stake. A few bucks, maybe, but not more than that.

Not until now.

She could always say no. Remembering that, she tossed down a five of spades and picked up the jack of clubs that was showing. Her hand was improving, but it still wasn't great.

"Gin."

Lauren looked up, startled. "Already?"

"'Fraid so." With a smile, he spread out his cards. Straight diamonds, from king on down.

"I guess your luck really did change," Lauren said, staring at the cards. Was fate suddenly calling the shots? Had it been all along?

"Care to try again?" he asked.

She was tempted, but a little voice far in the back of her mind prevented her. Softly, she said, "A bet's a bet."

He stood, gathered the cards and put them away in the box. Holding out a hand, he said, "Come here."

A switch seemed to trip in Lauren. She didn't think, didn't question, didn't doubt. Instead, she simply stood and went to him. When his fingers curled around hers, she shivered slightly. Caution warred with desire and, behind it all, curiosity—wondering, marveling curiosity at how this could be happening to her and where it would lead.

She felt almost as though she was no longer fully in herself, but was standing off to the side watching another woman, an entirely different person. This stranger looked like her, but there the similarity ended. Surely that wasn't her being drawn closer to the tall, lean man with the pewter eyes and the unreadable expression?

The scent and warmth of him, his all-encompassing strength and virility, filled her. She shut her eyes for an instant. When she opened them again, he was looking directly at her.

"I may not remember much," he said quietly, "but I do know that I've never met anyone like you before."

She managed a faint, nervous smile. "A nurse or a bad cardplayer?"

"A woman," he said, "a strong, brave beautiful woman." His breath touched her cheek. "Now about what I want—"

She could say no. Even if they hadn't agreed to that up front, it was always her absolute right. There was just one problem. Would she actually want to?

"A back rub," John said. "A really good, bone-deep back rub. I feel as though I'm tied up in knots."

"Back rub?" She was not disappointed, absolutely not, she told herself.

"Unless you don't want to, of course."

"That's okay. I've given my share of back rubs."

His eyebrows lifted ever so slightly. "I'll bet you're good at it, too."

"Good? I'm great. Step over here, sir." She pointed to the couch.

He went. Unbuttoning his shirt, he said, "I want you to know I really appreciate this."

She nodded absently as his shirt came off. Against the whiteness of the bandages, the broad sweep of his chest was dark, ribbed with muscle, softened by a fine dusting of hair. Actually, there was a whole lot more chest to see than bandages. He'd put on far less than she would have, probably to lessen the pain when the time came to remove them.

"You'll have to lie down," Lauren said. Her voice sounded odd, softer and less certain than normal.

He stretched out facedown on the couch. Lauren took a deep breath. It was only a back rub. Just the sort of kind but impersonal service anyone would do for a fellow human being.

Right.

At the first touch of his body beneath her hands, a deep shudder coursed through her. She took a quick breath, fighting against a wave of sensation, none of it kind but impersonal. Sweet Lord, what was happening to her? She had more sense than this. Didn't she?

Back rub. Very simple. The only trick was to apply enough pressure to ease the muscles without inflicting any bruising. But then the notion that she could bruise him was almost laughable. He seemed all tensile strength and hard, unyielding power, the very epitome of all that was different from herself.

Never had she been so aware of the contrast between male and female. The edge of the couch where she perched might as well have been a precipice. She felt as though she was in real danger of falling, but why and into what she had no idea.

Slowly, her hands began to move. His skin was warm and smooth, vibrant with life. She pressed her lips together hard and tried to concentrate.

"That feels great," John murmured. She could see him in profile, long lashes lying against one lean cheek. His eyes were closed. He looked thoroughly and completely relaxed.

Damn him. She could barely breathe and he seemed about to fall asleep. Talk about unfair.

Still, the appearance was deceptive. She could feel the tension in his corded muscles. No wonder he'd wanted a back rub.

"Better?" she asked.

"Much. I don't think I've ever felt this tied up in knots."

"Gosh, I wonder why? Could it have something to do with what you've been through?"

"Getting shot, not knowing who I am, fearing the worst?"

"That's right."

"Gee, you think maybe I'm overly sensitive?"

"I don't know. Let's find out." On an impulse she could scarcely credit, Lauren lightly brushed her fingers down his sides beginning just below his arms. Instantly, he jerked.

"You're ticklish." She was quite pleased by her discovery.

"Cut that out."

"Sorry. I don't know what came over me."

Moments later it happened again. She could have sworn she hadn't done anything but there was no getting around it—he was extremely ticklish.

Also fast. She didn't have a moment's warning before he rolled over and grabbed both her hands in his. His eyes glittered. She found herself staring at the hard line of his mouth. "You're asking for trouble," he warned.

There was that feeling again of not being quite herself. It was growing stronger, enveloping her. She heard her own voice as though from a great distance. "It seems to me that I've been doing that for a while now."

His hold on her tightened, then abruptly eased, although he did not let go of her completely. "It's late. I'll take the couch tonight."

That was her cue. Stand, say good-night, go to bed. Tomorrow was another day. Tomorrow and tomorrow... stretching out before her, safe, predictable, utterly unappealing.

She gathered up all the doubts, concerns and fears, all the wariness that had dogged her throughout her life, grim cousin to the same drive that had made her succeed, bundled them into a hard little kernel and felt them turn to dust within her.

"That would be a shame," she said as the wind blew outside and night wrapped around them. "It's such a big bed."

Chapter 12

Somewhere he'd read that men and women had diametrically different approaches to sex. Presented with an opportunity, a man—lacking a real commitment to another woman and sometimes even then—would always choose to take advantage of a sexual opportunity.

Women were a whole lot more choosy. It had to do with reproductive strategies, even when both parties did their level best to prevent any sort of reproduction from actually occurring. Regardless, the approaches were always different.

But not this time. While he lacked any precise memory of his previous sexual encounters, he knew he had never felt this way before. She was the first, the only woman who woke him to needs he couldn't deny or ignore.

Yet still he hesitated. There were all the doubts he had about himself, the terrible self-loathing that lurked at the edges of his consciousness every moment. What if he was what he feared, a man with no morality, no honor, no concern for others? How could he possibly allow her to become intimately involved with such a person?

But if he was, why would he care? Why wouldn't he just take advantage of what she offered?

No answer presented itself. Or if it did, he couldn't hear it over the roar of desire that threatened to drown out all else. She was so pliant in his arms, so womanly. He sat up, drawing her to him. The slender length of her fitted perfectly against his own far larger and more muscled frame. He ran his hands through her down-soft curls, tilting her head back....

Her mouth was sweet and hot, yielding beneath his. He hesitated, filled with an aching need to protect her, to cherish her, yet at the same time to possess her ruthlessly and totally. She made a small sound deep in her throat and wrapped her arms around his neck.

That gesture, so simple, so evocative, snapped the thin line of control he had managed to maintain. Without thought for his bandaged chest, he swept her up in his arms and climbed the narrow stairs to the loft.

Laying her on the bed, he came down swiftly on top of her, catching both her hands in his, lifting them above her head. His mouth devoured hers, his tongue thrusting deep and hard. He couldn't get enough of the taste and scent, the feel, of her. Like a starving man, he consumed her, his lips searching over the curve of her jaw, down the delicate line of her throat, along the opening of the absurdly big shirt she wore.

With one hand he undid the buttons and spread the two sides of the shirt apart. Her skin was slightly flushed, but still so fair that he could see the pale blue tracings of veins beneath, carrying her life's blood.

The lacy scrap of a bra she wore hid little from his eyes, yet any barrier between them was rapidly becoming intolerable. He slid his hand around her back and undid the clasp. Lifting her up slightly, he stripped away shirt and bra together and looked at her.

Her breasts were small, perfectly formed, the nipples tinted a rich, deep rose. They hardened under his eyes. He made a sound deep in his throat and bent over, taking her nipple into his mouth, rolling his tongue over it again and again.

She stiffened, her fingers tightening their hold in his hair, and whispered his name. They twined together on the wide, welcoming bed. He released her hands and moved his to the tie that served as her belt. He felt like a boy again, the boy he couldn't remember being, but who was reborn inside him. Few were the second chances any man received. Silently, he vowed he would find a way to make the most of his.

The tie gave way. He pulled it free and slid the slacks down her long, slim legs. She lay naked except for her tiny bikini panties. He put his fingers beneath the elastic sides and eased that last fragment of modesty from her.

The beauty of this woman—and the burning hunger of his own desire—robbed him of breath. He swept his hands over her, from her ankles over the smoothness of her thighs to the chalice of her hips and the indentation of her narrow waist to finally cup her breasts in his callused palms. The gesture was all-encompassing, claiming. He intended to know her completely, nothing held back, nothing denied.

He watched, fascinated, as small white teeth bit down on her lower lip. A growl of protest rose in him. He could not permit even so small a self-inflicted hurt.

His mouth took hers again, his tongue soothing the tiny wound before stroking her own. At the same time, he raised himself slightly and stripped off his remaining clothes. He was already fully aroused. When her fingers brushed him tentatively, he had to grit his teeth to keep from crying out. Quickly, he grabbed her hand and raised it to his lips.

''Easy,'' he murmured, smiling down into her eyes. Her cheeks were flushed, her gaze gleaming with the same dark passions he felt within himself. Rubbing his thumbs over her nipples, he slid his thigh between hers and began opening her to him.

She was petal soft, hot and wet. A groan wrenched from him. He knew sex, had done it before, understood it as much as anyone else. Yet this was also entirely new to him, an undiscovered land in which all things seemed possible.

A land in which he was no longer alone.

Heat roared through him. He was engulfed, consumed. Far in the distance, he heard himself call her name. The sound was harsh, alien, the voice of a man for whom control was fast fading.

Her hands stroked down the length of his back, cupping his buttocks. She squeezed lightly and raised her hips, rotating them against him.

Breath shuddering, he spread her legs wider and eased himself into her. At the first touch of her womanhood around him, a red mist seemed to move before his eyes. The last thin threads of his restraint snapped.

Lauren gasped. Her body was so tightly drawn that it felt as though every individual cell strummed to a rhythm she had never before heard or so much as imagined. The stranger who had been stirring within her almost from the moment she met John was a stranger no longer. It had become her true self, passionate, unbridled, heedless of the constraints of a lifetime.

The sensation of him within her was at once shocking and enthralling. She moved, tentatively at first, then with growing boldness, drawing him deeper.

His features above her were fiercely drawn, as though etched by the finest edged sword. He was darkly flushed, his eyes glittering. What tiny fragments of reason remained told her that she should be afraid, but she was completely beyond that. Even as he thrust harder and harder, claiming her, she felt only intense, overwhelming joy.

He slid his hands under her and raised her to him, thrusting again and again, deeper and deeper, his rhythm increasing until there was only the ruthless, almost savage reality of him at the very core of her being. The world and everything in it were blotted out.

There was only exquisite, blazing sensation spreading all through her, incandescent in its intensity.

She gasped, hardly breathing, as the sensation built and built, finally cresting within her so intensely that she screamed.

He followed a moment later, searing her with his heat and power, his life. Her name on his lips was half prayer, half incantation.

Deep in the night, John awoke. He had been dreaming, but couldn't remember what about. Thrown back into consciousness, he sat up with a jerk and looked around the darkened loft.

His heart pounded beneath his ribs. Real fear tore through him and he had no idea why. He had the sense of himself in desperate flight from something, but whatever it was, the knowledge slipped from him even as awareness returned.

He took a deep breath and willed himself to calm down. Slowly, his surroundings swam into focus. The clouds had cleared. By the first gray light of dawn he could make out the contours of the loft and, just beyond the railing, the main room of the cabin.

He remembered. In the same instant, he inhaled her evocative scent. Turning, he brushed a hand over her bare arm, needing to convince himself that she was real.

And there beside him, lying on her side, her lips slightly parted in sleep. One hand was curled beneath her chin, the other lay stretched toward him. Her hair was slightly tousled, her cheeks flushed. When he moved the sheet down a little, he saw a tiny reddening on the curve of one breast.

That small mark, so inconsequential that it could easily have gone unnoticed, banished the last lingering remnants of the dream. Whatever it had been, it was reality that mattered.

The memory of what they had shared stole over him like a warm, potent caress. With it came astonishment. Had all that incandescent passion truly happened?

Only the lingering satiation of his body and the clarity of the images in his mind assured him that it had. A faint smile curved his mouth. On this score at least, he had no difficulty at all remembering.

But not without a price. No sooner had the jumble of impressions, sensations and fragments of what he had seen, heard and felt rippled through his mind than hard on them came the renewing of desire. His body stirred, sudden and insistent in its demand.

He tried to resist his arousal. She was so deeply asleep, after all, and, besides, for all he knew she regretted what had happened between them. The thought of that pierced him. He hesitated in the act of reaching for her.

At that moment, Lauren stirred slightly. Her lashes fluttered. She looked up into his eyes.

And smiled. A slow, sensual, purely feminine smile accompanied by a long, languorous stretch.

"Morning," she murmured.

He smiled, too, from the sheer pleasure of watching her and from relief. "Barely."

She glanced toward the end of the loft rail. Her eyes looked heavy, slumberous, but the glance she shot him was entirely alert. "Maybe we should go back to sleep."

"Maybe."

"Or we could have breakfast."

"Good idea, and go for a hike."

"A little dip in the lake."

"Skinny-dip?"

She shivered. "Ooooh, cold."

"We can't have that," John said, the soul of consideration, and gathered her to him.

"Still cold?" he asked a long time later.

"What's cold?" Her voice was faint, tinged with utter satiation. She nestled against him, her skin like warm silk, and promptly fell back asleep.

He remained awake, staring up at the ceiling, wondering what it would take to keep this woman who had come like an unexpected gift into his life. Wondering, too, if he had any right to do so.

Chapter 13

"**I** think I should call someone to say I'm okay," Lauren said. They were sitting at the table finishing a late brunch. Outside, the sun shone brilliantly, but there was a cold snap to the air. The fire John had started was welcome.

"That's a good idea. Who did you have in mind?"

"A supervisor at St. Mary's. I just don't like the idea of them worrying about me."

He nodded toward the desk. "That phone's working. I checked."

"I'll have to keep it short in case anyone tries to trace it."

"That's a lot harder than it looks on television. You have to be set up for it to start with, and then it takes at least three minutes, usually more. Does the hospital have caller ID?"

"Not yet. There's talk about putting it in at least for the emergency room, but it hasn't happened so far."

"Then there shouldn't be any problem."

Lauren nodded slowly. She put down her fork and studied him. It was on the tip of her tongue to ask him how he knew the length of time required to trace a phone call, but she stopped herself. The last thing she wanted to do just then was arouse more concerns in him about who—and what—he was. That kind of information was something a drug dealer anxious to avoid detection would be likely to know. Truth be told, she didn't want to think about it herself.

Indeed, she was having difficulty thinking about anything other than the night they had shared. Every moment of it seemed to still resonate within her. She felt transformed in a way she could scarcely credit.

But with that happiness had come an unavoidable sense of guilt for what she had so far managed to overlook, namely that there were people who cared about her and would be worrying.

While John cleared the table, she placed the call. As it rang, she silently rehearsed what she would say. She was still in the midst of that when the call went through.

"Morrissey."

"Martha, I'm glad I reached you. It's Lauren."

"Lauren? Oh, my God, Lauren! Where are you? We've all been worried sick. The police—"

"Listen, I can't talk very long. I just wanted to let you know that I'm all right. I'm sorry to have gone off like I did, but there didn't seem to be any other way—"

"What do you mean? Lauren, listen to me, whatever's going on, you've got to come back here. The FBI's all over the place, talking to everyone who knows you, trying to get any lead on where you could be. You *and* John Doe. He forced you to leave, didn't he?"

"Yes, but— The FBI—?"

"They still have no idea who he is, Lauren, or why he did this. Honey, if you can really talk, tell me where you are."

"I can't— Martha, I'm sorry. I have to go."

"No, don't! Where are you—?"

Lauren's hand shook as she hung up the phone. She felt sick to her stomach. The FBI was at St. Mary's. She should have anticipated that. After all, they would view her disappearance as a kidnapping case. But what if Becker and Hollis were real agents?

What if she had made a terrible mistake?

She turned away from the phone. John was standing at the kitchen sink, his back to her. She studied the long, strong line of his body and remembered how it had felt against her own, how he had touched her, the things he had said and done, what he had made her feel. Somewhere in all of that, passion and reason had to intersect. She couldn't separate the two and was smart enough not to try. But she also understood that they were different. She could no more be ruled by one than ignore the other.

"Everything all right?" he asked as he put the last dish away. He stood at the sink, a dishcloth in his hands, wearing khakis and a flannel shirt, his hair glistening from the shower he had taken. His eyes were gentle on her, his features relaxed.

Slowly, she nodded. "They're worried, of course. My friend says the FBI is all over the place."

He didn't seem surprised. "You can be out of New York City in fifteen minutes if traffic's not too bad. They'd have to figure you could be across state lines."

"And once you are, the FBI is involved?"

"Right. But they're called in on almost all kidnappings even if there's no concrete evidence that the victim's been taken out of state. It's one of the bureau's real areas of expertise."

"Interesting," Lauren murmured. Either he had some practical experience in the area of kidnapping, or he had an unusual degree of familiarity with the workings of the FBI.

He hung the towel on a drying rack and glanced out the window. "Looks like a great day. How about a ride into town?"

"Are you sure that's a good idea?"

John shrugged. "I figure I lived here at least for a while. The locals must know me. Maybe I can pick up some useful information."

"Fine with me, then. It would be nice to get fresh food, too."

She accepted his offer of a jacket before they left the cabin. It was definitely turning colder.

The town of Appleton lay nestled between mountains a short but crucial distance off the interstate. Those few miles enabled it to maintain a certain New England authenticity without jeopardizing the all-important tourist dollars.

The main street was lined with clapboard shops and houses, all two stories high and painted in bright colonial blues, reds and yellows. Attractive wooden signs hung from wrought-iron hooks above each store. Flowerpots filled with ivy hung from lampposts or framed doorways. Obviously, every effort had been made to keep the town looking picturesque rather than tacky.

So far as Lauren was concerned, it worked. Getting out of the car, she stopped for a moment to look up and down the street. When they'd driven through before, it had been night and she'd seen little. But now she could fully appreciate Appleton's charm. City girl that she was, it was a place she could imagine herself living.

"It's lovely," she said as John joined her on the sidewalk.

He pocketed the car keys. "Seems farther than just a few hundred miles from New York, doesn't it?"

"Like another planet. Is that why you chose to live here?"

"Perhaps." He took her arm and gestured toward a small supermarket. "How about we start there?"

Lauren agreed. She felt almost unbearably domestic as she followed John around while he pushed the shopping cart. What little grocery shopping she did for herself was always on the run—a quart of milk and a box of cereal picked up at the all-night convenience store, that sort of thing. She'd eaten most of her meals at the hospital simply because she was there so much, and when she did get back to her apartment she was usually far too tired to cook.

This was different. She realized that the moment he hefted a honeydew melon, tested it for softness and held it out for her to sniff. She did, but tentatively. What was it supposed to smell like, anyway?

"That would be okay for tomorrow, don't you think?" he asked.

"Oh, sure, tomorrow." Or next week, next month. How would she know?

"What kind of tomatoes do you like?"

She was about to say red ones when she realized that the store also sold the yellow variety, which she'd glimpsed from time to time but had never taken seriously enough to buy. There were also cherry tomatoes, plum tomatoes, hydroponic tomatoes and others she'd never heard of before.

"Those look fine," she said, pointing at random.

John frowned. "You think so? How about these?" He expertly plucked a cluster of perfectly ripened specimens still attached to their vines from the display.

"Or those," Lauren said.

"Do you like endive?"

Endive...endive...oh, right, Belgian lettuce, sort of. A little bitter but not bad.

"Love it."

"Me, too. How about a little radicchio to make it interesting?"

"Perfect."

They made it through fruits and vegetables, but ahead lay meat and poultry. Who knew what he would find there?

"The duck looks good," John said, peering into the case.

"Best I've seen."

"There's currant sauce in the freezer at the cabin," he said as he selected several lucky ducks. "That should go good with these."

"What's duck without currant sauce, is what I always say."

"A lot of people do prefer orange sauce, it being more traditional."

"But a bit tired, wouldn't you say?"

"Definitely. That reminds me, where's the orange juice . . . ?"

Lauren was about to point to the case that held tidy little cans waiting to be opened, the just-add-water-and-stir variety. But John was off in the opposite direction, toward the small, hand-lettered sign that read Fresh Squeezed.

She should have known. Whoever this guy was, he definitely had not been living on fast food and microwave meals.

Maybe his mother had taught him to cook, she of the five sons and the progressive attitudes. If so, they'd dined well in the Santos house.

She was still thinking about that, puzzling over the sort of background he seemed to have come from, as John tossed a few extra things into the cart. The supermarket was almost empty at the moment. Only one cash register was open. The woman waiting there glanced up as they approached. Her broad face creased in a smile.

"Well, hi, there, Mr. Putnam. We haven't seen you in a while."

Chapter 14

John froze. He stared at the woman. Instinct took over and he managed to smile, but he knew it was strained. "It's nice to see you, too," he said.

She nodded, busy running items over the scanner. "Turned a bit cold, wouldn't you say?"

"Definitely. It looks like you've been having a nice spring here."

"Oh, it's been coming on slow, though, this year." She laughed. "Of course, with that winter we had, we can't say we're surprised, can we?"

"I guess not. The winter was pretty rough."

"Rough? I should say. 'Course I didn't hear you skiers complaining none."

She knew he skied. That seemed to indicate he'd been in Appleton during the winter.

"There's such a thing as too much snow even for us," he said.

"Oh, that's right. I forgot. You were here when those poor tourists ran off the road in their four-wheel drive. You climbed down to help get them out, didn't you?"

John shrugged. He had absolutely no memory of such an incident and had to hope that he merely looked modest.

"How did they make out?" he asked.

"Fine, far as I know. Lucky thing for them you guys were there. Done much climbing lately?"

"No, not recently."

The last of the groceries was bagged. John paid and pocketed his change.

"Have a nice day," the woman said. She gave Lauren a quick once-over and started checking out the next customer.

They crossed the street in silence to where they had left the car. John unlocked the trunk and put the groceries in. As he slammed the lid, Lauren said, "You realize she may have simply mistaken you for someone else."

"She didn't seem to have any doubts about who she was talking to—and there is ski gear in the cabin."

"I'd bet there's ski gear in every house around here. That proves nothing."

John sighed. He tucked his hands into his pockets and looked at her. Very gently, he said, "We've got to face facts. It seems I've been living here under an assumed name, or at least it isn't the name that's on my driver's license."

"Do you remember what she was talking about, when the people drove off the road?"

"No, but then there's a great deal I don't remember. Virtually my whole life, for instance. Except for a few scattered images, I might as well have been hatched right there on that sidewalk in New York."

It was a compelling notion. The gunman in shadows, his face hidden, the gun blazing and himself falling, shot through by fire, breaking apart to be reborn as—what? John Santos? Mr. Putnam? Who were they?

Who was he?

"You know you had brothers," Lauren reminded him, "and a mother. You know you like to cook and you're just a bit of a sports nut."

"I know about guns, too. Don't forget that. And I know how to run from the cops. Face it, Lauren, this is looking worse, not better."

She wasn't ready to admit that. "Why? Because you've lived here under a different name? Okay, that's unusual, but there are people who do it. Celebrities, for example."

"Criminals, for another."

She shook her head. "You're jumping to conclusions."

He stared at her, absorbing the conviction in her face. This was a strong, intelligent woman who lived entirely in the real world and knew it for what it was. Yet, she was choosing to believe in him. A wave of emotion washed through him—surprise, gratitude and something else. Something very powerful, very new, stirring inside him.

His hand brushed her cheek gently. "You're beautiful, Lauren Walters, inside and out." A low chuckle broke from him as color washed over her pale skin.

For a moment, their eyes met. Lauren was the first to glance away. "Let's find out if anyone here knows you," she said and took his hand.

There was a coffee shop about half a block away. They went inside, welcomed by the aroma of freshly ground beans and assorted pastries. Several people were seated at the small tables in the front, reading or talking among themselves.

Lauren and John went to the counter to order. The clerk was a young man of about twenty. He finished steaming a metal pitcher of milk and smiled.

"May I help you?"

There wasn't a flicker of recognition on his face. Whoever he was, he didn't appear to know either John Santos or Mr. Putnam.

They ordered cappuccinos and carried them over to a table that was free by the door. Seated, they stared out the windows at the people passing by. There weren't many of them. With the ski season over and the summer not yet begun, Appleton was a quiet place.

"Do you remember anything about this place?" Lauren asked. "I mean, besides the cabin?"

"I'm not sure— I think there's a school just west of here with large playing fields out in front, but I could be wrong."

"Anything else?"

"Not really—"

"No, come on, you're thinking of something."

He shrugged, then took a sip of the coffee. It was good, also familiar. He had done this before, sat in a place like this, drinking coffee. But not with a woman like Lauren. On that point, at least, he was quite sure.

"I have an impression of skiing, going down a trail very fast, snow flying, a feeling of exhilaration. But it could have been anywhere, possibly not even in this country." The moment he said it, he knew he was right. He liked to ski, had done so often, in a wide variety of places including other countries.

He'd traveled a great deal on business, but also for pleasure.

"It just occurred to me," he said, "there doesn't seem to be a passport at the cabin."

"Or many personal papers at all."

"Maybe we haven't looked hard enough."

He nodded, but he was thinking more along the lines that the papers were locked up somewhere else. His passport, bank statements, credit cards, all the usual paraphernalia of their society—they existed, they were real. He just couldn't find them.

Or was it that he didn't want to?

The thought sprung unbidden into his mind. If he was what he feared, how much more pleasant it would be to keep that part of himself buried and to be instead this Mr. Putnam who owned the cabin outside of Appleton, who crewed, played tennis, skied, who played the Good Samaritan.

Who might just possibly deserve Lauren Walters.

"What are you thinking?" she asked softly.

He looked up, suddenly seeing himself in the mirror of her eyes, a tense, preoccupied man fighting very unpleasant possibilities.

"That being this guy Putnam might be okay."

"We don't even know that Putnam exists."

"Then let's try to find out," he said and rose.

They walked a short distance down the street, past several boutiques, a hardware store and a dry cleaner. The shopfronts gave way to houses. Several children biked past, bundled up in winter jackets. A woman strolled by with a shopping cart. She gave no sign of recognizing him.

On impulse, he stopped where a small side road angled off the main street. "Let's see what's down here."

The road led down a small hill. At the bottom, almost hidden behind wild rhododendron bushes, was a small but perfectly detailed house. A peaked roof was trimmed with gingerbread painted yellow in contrast to the cheerful spring green of the building itself. Shutters also painted yellow framed each of the four front windows, two upstairs, two downstairs. The door was white but decorated from top to bottom with a painting of a sunflower. There was a little garden out in front just beginning to stir to life.

A flagstone path led around the back of the house. John started down it.

"What is this?" Lauren asked, following.

"I don't know—at least, I'm not sure. But I've been here before. I know that." He was excited, pleased that he finally recognized something besides the cabin. The tiny, cheerful house had some special significance for him.

They could hear hammering. Around the back, hidden from view on the lane, was a small shed. Its double doors stood open. A young man was working out in front. He wore a brown leather apron and, as they watched, he laid a piece of metal on an anvil and struck it with the large hammer he held in his other hand.

"Liam—"

The name was out before John realized what he was saying. The man turned and glanced at them with obvious recognition. "Hi, there. I'll be with you in just a minute," he said and went back to striking the metal. Several blows later, he raised a flat, slightly curved strip of metal about two feet long and two inches wide. "That should do it."

"So," he said as he wiped his hands off on the apron, "what can I do for you?"

"Actually, we were just passing by and I wanted to show my friend here the shop," John said. "I hope you don't mind?"

Liam shook his head. He was an attractive man in his late twenties, well built with dark blond hair and blue eyes. The glance he gave Lauren was appreciative but respectful.

"Hey, you know I love to show the place off. Do you know much about crewing, Miss—"

"Laurie," she said quickly. "And you're…Liam?"

"That's right, courtesy of my Irish forebears. They built curraghs, I build sculls. I suppose it's pretty much the same thing."

"Sculls? Of course, I should have known. Did you build the one—" She faltered but caught herself, then took the plunge. "The one John has by the lake?"

"I did, indeed. Have you been out on her yet?"

"No, I haven't, but I'm looking forward to it."

"Flies over the water, she does." Liam went on, saying something about how the quality of the resin contributed to speed, but John barely heard him. He was absorbed by the fact that this man knew him, recognized him as John for whom he had built a custom scull. But John who?

"I was wondering," Lauren said. "Are there many Putnams around here?"

Liam frowned slightly. "It's an old New England name, right enough, but so far as I know, John's the only one in these parts."

So much for that. Here in Appleton he was John Putnam. Added to the guns, the disturbing memories and the growing fears about himself was the fact that he had two identities. It was enough to give a guy a complex.

They stayed awhile longer, Lauren clearly apprehensive that one of them would say something wrong, a concern John fully shared. All the same, Liam seemed to find nothing amiss. He saw them off cheerfully before going back to his hammering.

"John Putnam," Lauren said as they walked back up the hill to the main street. "It sounds almost Puritan."

"Somehow, I think that's misleading."

"Do you feel like a John Putnam?"

"As much as I feel like a John Santos."

"Neither one seems more real than the other?"

"I'm afraid not, which, of course, raises the possibility that they're both false identities."

"Or that they're both real."

He stopped and looked at her. The wind ruffled her hair gently and made her skin glow. But then, her skin did that normally. He resisted the urge to touch her again. "Come on, I'm all for trying to put a positive twist on things, but how could anyone have two legal names?"

"Maybe they're part of the same name. John Putnam Santos, for instance. Or John Santos Putnam."

"Putnam Santos. Santos Putnam. Either one would be unusual, that's for sure."

"But not impossible."

No, not impossible, and the odd thing was, the idea didn't feel all that outlandish. He tried them again, silently rolling the names around in his mind. Of the two possibilities, John Putnam Santos seemed the better fit.

They started walking again.

"If that really is my name, there's got to be a story there."

"Your mother was a Putnam. She came from an old line New England family and she was feisty, full of adventure. She met your father while traveling. He swept her off her feet. They fell madly in love, got married and settled down to raise a family."

John laughed. He couldn't help it; she sounded so serious. "And how did her family react to that?"

"They congratulated her on making such a good choice. His family did the same. They had a wonderful life."

"Until one of their sons got stabbed."

Lauren paled. "I'm sorry. That was stupid of me."

They had reached the car. She looked so appalled that John was struck with remorse. He had absolutely no right to remind her of his troubled thoughts. She deserved far better.

"No," he said, "I'm sorry. I can never thank you enough for what you've done for me, what you are doing. And instead I keep putting my foot in it. Forgive me?"

"Yes," she said simply.

He went very still, looking at her. There was no artifice about her, no trickery. She was as open and honest a person as he had ever met. A woman to be trusted—and cherished.

Silently, he drew her to him. There on the street in the small Vermont village he held her close and breathed a silent prayer that he would not have to let her go.

Chapter 15

Heading the car out of town, John had to wait a moment for a dark blue sedan making a left turn. Something about the guy behind the wheel struck him, but the impression was fleeting and he thought nothing more of it.

They returned to the cabin. Lauren insisted on checking his wounds. One thing led to another and it was several hours later before the ducks made it into the oven.

"Why two?" Lauren asked lazily. She was lying on the couch in front of the fire, a glass of wine in her hand. Wearing one of his flannel shirts and nothing else, she looked like a delectable urchin. Her short, feathery hair was slightly mussed. Her eyes were heavy lidded, slumberous in the aftermath of passion. The reflection of firelight on her long, bare legs drew his eye. He remembered how it had felt to lie between those satiny thighs, being drawn into her, and smiled. Faulty memory or not, he was certain he had never known a woman as enticing. Or one who so easily made him forget all else.

"Two? Oh, the ducks. One for dinner, the other for salad tomorrow."

Her eyebrows rose fractionally. "Salad?"

"Cold duck and wild-rice salad with a cranberry dressing."

"Of course, duck salad. I should have known." She set her wineglass down and rose from the couch, strolling toward him. She smiled as her gaze appraised his chest, bare above the khakis he'd pulled on.

"If you also do windows," Lauren said, "I may decide this is for real."

"You can hire people for that." He managed to slip the ducks back into the oven with one hand while wrapping the other around her. She felt so damn good, so warm and womanly. His need for her never seemed to ease. Already he was hard again, hungering for her.

He slid his hands up under the shirt, cupping her buttocks. She moved against him. Against his throat, she murmured, "How long to dinner?"

"Long enough." Lifting her, he wrapped her long legs around him and carried her into the living room. The couch was too narrow for what he had in mind. Kneeling, he laid her on the rug in front of the fire and came down on top of her.

The urgency of their passion stunned him. Their lovemaking this time should have been slow and gentle, but he knew any such thing was beyond him.

Hastily, he unbuttoned the flannel shirt and slipped it from her. She shivered, but not from cold. Already her nipples were hard, her breathing ragged.

He took her mouth with his, hard and fast, his tongue delving deeply. At the same time, he unclasped his pants and freed himself. Blood thrummed in his ears. He was seized by a wild, driving rhythm that drove out all reason, all hesitation.

His fingers found and stroked the silky cleft between her legs. To his infinite relief, she was hot and wet, as ready for him as he was for her. At his first thrust, she moaned, but her arms were tight around him, clasping her to him. He shut his eyes against the waves of passion that threatened to undo him and took a deep, shuddering breath. Slowly, with fierce tenderness, he moved within her, driving her higher and higher, letting the wildness take them both.

His tongue laved her nipples as his lower body moved, almost but never quite withdrawing, penetrating deeper and deeper until he felt the powerful, velvety convulsions begin all around him. She cried out, sobbing his name, her luminous features taut with release.

His own followed. Head back, hands clasping her hips to hold her to him, he thrust once more, and at last poured himself into her. His pleasure seemed endless.

Timeless moments later, he raised his head. Lauren lay beneath him, her eyes closed, her breathing gentled but still uneven. He could feel the fluttering beat of her heart against his own. Gently, he stroked the curve of her cheek.

Her lashes trembled. Slowly, she looked up at him. A faint smile lifted the corners of her mouth now swollen from his kisses. "Forget windows," she murmured. "I wouldn't want you to waste your strength."

He laughed. "Got a better use for it?"

"You could say that." She sighed deeply and snuggled against him. Her eyes fluttered, and her voice was low and faintly muffled. "I think I'll just go to sleep now."

Carefully, he stood and righted his clothes. She stirred slightly as he lifted her and laid her on the couch. Covering her with a quilt, he gazed down at her. The wave of tenderness that went through him was as fierce in its own way as the passion that had consumed him such a short time before. It shook him deeply.

He turned away and went into the kitchen. At the sink, he splashed cold water on his face. The thought of sleep was enticing, but he needed to reassert some level of control over himself.

Besides, the ducks would be ready soon.

Lauren woke to the tantalizing aromas of food and a sense of well-being so deep and all pervasive that she thought she was still dreaming. Only when she became aware of the couch fabric slightly scratching against her bare skin did she realize that she was very much awake.

Sitting up, she drew the quilt over her breasts and looked around. The fire was dancing merrily; candles gleamed on the table, reflecting off the long-stemmed glasses filled with a ruby wine.

Her stomach growled. She grimaced, marveling at how she seemed to have become driven by appetites of all sorts. Swinging her legs over the side of the couch, she stood.

"Everything all right?" John asked. He stepped out of the shadows by the kitchen, startling her.

She jumped slightly and found she had difficulty meeting his eyes. Their unbridled lovemaking had left her feeling uncommonly self-conscious. She felt dazed and almost disbelieving, as though it had all happened to someone else. Even her voice sounded different, gentler somehow, more tentative. "Fine . . . I'll just go freshen up."

Grabbing the shirt she'd been wearing, she beat a hasty retreat. In the bathroom, she took a quick shower and towel dried her hair. The temptation to put on more clothes—a full suit of body armor if she'd had it—was strong, but she resisted, unwilling to show the extent of her discomfort.

No, that was too strong a word. In point of fact, she was luxuriously, seductively, sensuously content. Every atom of her body seemed to be doing its best to purr.

And therein lay the problem. She was not a content sort of person, never had been. She'd always counted on a certain fine edge of tension to get her through life. Now that seemed to have melted.

Maybe a little food would make her feel better.

Lauren grimaced and stuck out her tongue at herself in the mirror above the sink. Who was she kidding? A little candlelit dinner *à deux* with the world's most perfect man—except for forgetting who he was and thinking maybe he was a drug dealer, but otherwise perfect—was not going to restore her equilibrium. Far from it.

All the same, a girl had to eat. Taking a deep breath, she steeled herself for the ordeal ahead.

It was just the teeniest bit distracting watching the candlelight flicker over his bare chest, she thought a short time later as they sat across from each other, the duck neatly portioned out, music playing softly in the background. But then it was such a nice chest, every muscle and sinew so well defined, the skin sun warmed and just enough of a dusting of dark, curling hair to make it interesting. Sort of like icing on the cake.

Yeah, right. Sort of like nothing she'd ever before encountered would be closer to it. She was in over her head and sinking fast. The problem was that she was also enjoying it. Immensely.

"Hungry?" John asked.

"Ravenous." She raised her glass, trying to ignore the warmth washing over her face. Hungry in all sorts of ways. Insatiable. "To the chef," she said.

He raised his own glass, touching hers lightly. Their fingers brushed. She drew her hand away. The wine was full and heady, evocative of sun-drenched fields beneath cobalt skies, dusted with the clouds that brought swift, cooling rains to splatter over the ripening fruit and into the dark, fertile earth.

The music wrapped around them. Lauren took a bite of the duck, closing her eyes in sheer delight. She opened them to find John watching her, his gaze silvered with lambent fires.

"You're spoiling me."

"I prefer to think of it as pampering."

"I don't believe I've ever been pampered." She sounded apprehensive.

"Don't worry, it won't hurt."

Oh, but it would when all this ended and she had to go back to the real world, as she would have to eventually and would be very wise to remember. But not just yet. Not while the music played and the fire burned, and all things seemed possible, if only briefly.

Later. She would think about all that later.

For the moment—

"What would you like to do after dinner?" he asked.

Her smile told him.

Chapter 16

Deep in the night, John awoke. The transition from sleep to consciousness was abrupt. One moment he was dreaming. The next, he was startlingly, almost painfully alert.

Billy Panos.

Billy get-in-my-face-and-I'll-off-you Panos.

Billy who liked to cut up whores and was rumored to use a tad too much of his own product. John could see him as clearly as though he was standing at the foot of the bed, going on about somebody he'd killed, strutting. Big man.

But not above running an errand for the bigger men, reminding them of just how useful he could be.

Billy Panos. Driving a dark blue sedan with three other guys in it through picturesque, downtown Appleton.

He sat up, got out of bed and walked over to the loft window. His stomach twisted and he could feel cold sweat on his back. He knew Billy Panos as surely as he knew anything. He could describe him down to the scar that cut across the left side of his throat and the missing knuckle of his left index finger, bitten off, it was said in a fight years back.

At that precise moment, he knew Billy Panos better than he knew himself.

And he knew Billy's being in Appleton was definitely not good news.

How in hell had they found him? Where had he slipped up? What had he forgotten?

A harsh laugh broke from him. He'd forgotten damn near everything. Knowing that, how had he believed he wouldn't slip up somewhere along the line and leave himself wide open to the same enemies who had already tried to kill him once?

And they had tried to kill him. He was damn sure of that. Getting shot down on a New York City street had not been a random act of violence. He'd been set up. He'd even suspected it. That was why he was moving around without ID, why he had the guns in the back of the car.

He'd come into town to do what? Get something? Speak to someone? Knowing he was taking a chance but thinking the risk was worthwhile. He'd been too cocky for his own good and it had almost gotten him killed.

But now it wasn't just him he had to worry about.

Now there was Lauren.

He looked at her asleep, her hair tousled, the covers down far enough to expose the long, slender line of her back. An aching sense of vulnerability filled him. Alone, he could stand and face any danger. But he wasn't alone anymore. He had to protect her.

Had to. At all costs.

He let her sleep while he went downstairs, put on coffee and then dressed. Frost rimmed the ground outside. He pulled on two pairs of socks and boots, then stuffed extra clothes into a pack.

She stirred just as he was finishing getting ready. Going over to the bed, he sat down beside her and waited until she opened her eyes. Seeing him, a slow, languorous smile crept over her face.

"You're up early," she said.

He touched her hair lightly, hating what he had to tell her. Hating the whole damn situation. "We've got a problem."

Lauren dressed quickly. At John's direction, she put on long winter underwear that was miles too big, corduroy pants, a flannel shirt, a sweater and enough pairs of socks to be able to fit her feet into a pair of his boots without walking out of them. It was a little hard doing all that in almost complete darkness—John had said not to turn any lights on. When she was done, she felt like a cross between a mummy and an astronaut, but she didn't argue. The look in his eyes had said it all.

She came downstairs to find him stuffing food and a first-aid kit into the pack by the glow of a small flashlight. "Can you manage this?" he asked, handing the pack to her.

She hefted it and nodded. "It's fine, but what's it all for?"

"Nothing, I hope."

Without explanation, he went to the closet near the front door and began removing the guns from it. Lauren gasped when she realized how many there were. John swung one across his back and stuck another in his waistband.

"Can you handle any of these?" he asked.

Lauren shook her head. Having seen firsthand the damage guns could do, she'd never felt any inclination to learn how to use one. Now she had to wonder if she should regret that decision.

"I thought we were just going to drive out of town," she said. "Go someplace else while we figure out what to do."

John began loading one of the guns. Without looking up, he said, "Sounds good to me."

"Then why all this?"

"Just in case Billy's got other ideas."

"You know you could be wrong. It might not even be him. Even if he was the man you saw, he may have left by now."

He shrugged. "Could be."

"But you don't think so?"

He finished what he was doing and leaned the gun against the wall. With no wasted motion, he began loading another. "Billy Panos gets to wear three-thousand-dollar suits and wash down his nose candy with vintage champagne because he gets the job done. He doesn't walk away. That was him in the car. He's here in Appleton, looking for me. Before he discovers that John Santos is John Putnam, we're going to get out of here.''

"You're remembering more."

"Yeah, and none of it good." He reached for a hunting jacket, then put it on. "I want you to wait here. I should be back in half an hour tops. If I'm not, or if you hear any shooting, call 911, then get the hell out of here. Hide in the woods until the police come."

She paled. Her eyes were wide and dark. "What are you talking about—shooting? Where are you going?"

"To check the road." He picked up one of the guns. "Billy likes to work at night. I just want to make sure he's not already out there."

"We'll go together in the car."

"Once I'm sure the road's clear." He laid a hand on her arm gently. "It's okay, everything's going to be all right. I'll be back soon."

She pressed her lips together and nodded. He gave her a quick smile he hoped was reassuring and slipped out the door.

It had turned very cold. The sky was heavy with clouds. He sniffed the air and frowned. This late in the season, it was rare to get snow but not impossible.

He moved into the darkness of the trees beside the road, the gun gripped lightly in both hands. Breaking into a swift, smooth run, he covered a quarter mile before he stopped to look and listen. Nothing. Except for the usual night sounds of the forest, the world seemed entirely still.

Moving on, he was more than halfway from the cabin to the main road when he suddenly stopped. For just an instant, he thought he'd heard something. He waited, not breathing, until the sound came again.

Voices. The far off murmur of men talking. He couldn't make out anything they were saying, or even judge how much farther away they were. But he was sure they were there.

Crouching, he continued more slowly, pausing every few yards to listen. The voices grew more distinct. He heard laughter.

Where the main road met the road to the cabin, there was a small rise. John crawled up it on his belly, glad that his clothes were dark and the night moonless. Peering over the edge, he saw what he had feared most.

The blue sedan was parked right at the bottom of the cabin road. Two men were outside it, smoking and talking as they moved around to keep warm. Two others were still seated in the car. As John watched, another vehicle pulled up beside the first. A man got out and went over to speak to the men in the sedan. He nodded, as though receiving instructions.

Three other men got out of the second vehicle. They spoke briefly with the first man, then quickly spread out, heading into the woods along the road. Forming a cordon to cut off retreat, no doubt.

Another in the original group took something from the back of the car and, with what looked like amused encouragement from his associates, began shinnying up a utility pole to cut the phone line.

Very thorough, very professional. And unmistakable.

Billy Panos had found him. If he followed his usual course, he would wait a short while more until his men were all in place and he figured John would be deeply asleep, then make his move.

Cursing silently, John inched down the rise. When he reached the bottom, he straightened up cautiously. As quickly as he could without making any noise, he headed back toward the cabin.

Lauren checked her watch again. The dial glowed luminescent in the dark. John had been gone twenty-five minutes. She'd heard nothing, but that didn't reassure her. Fear lay like a lead weight in her stomach.

If something happened to him—how could she possibly deal with that? She, who had worked in emergency rooms that resembled war zones, could not bear the thought of him being hurt again. The possibility alone was enough to bring her close to tears.

Please, God, let him be all right. Please let this all be nothing. Please let Billy Panos and everyone like him disappear off the face of the earth. Please.

She took a deep breath and looked at her watch again. Twenty-seven minutes. He'd said a half hour. He'd practically promised. What if there was a gun with a silencer? What if he was already—

A sob broke from her. She couldn't stand this. Anything would be better. The guns were all gone from the closet. That was just as well; she would probably have ended up shooting herself.

But that didn't mean she could just go on waiting, hiding, praying everything would be all right.

She opened the cabin door and stepped outside. If only it weren't so dark—but, no, that would be more dangerous for John. If that still mattered. If he was all right. If—

Another sob broke from her. She started down the road with no clear plan, only the overwhelming need to find him, to assure herself that he was unharmed or, if it was too late for that, to share whatever had happened to him.

A shadow stepped out of the deeper shadow of the trees. She realized it too late, started to scream—

A hard hand clamped over her mouth, an arm like steel wrapping around her, pulling her into the darkness near the cabin.

"Be quiet," John said. "Panos is down the road and he's not alone."

Lauren sagged with relief. She wanted to throw her arms around him, kiss him forever, and at the same time slap him silly for terrifying her like that. But he was right. If Billy Panos was there and she had cried out—

"I'm sorry," she whispered when John released his hand. "I was just so worried about you."

He held her tight against him for a moment, then pushed her back against the outside wall of the cabin. "Stay here. I need to get a few more things."

He was back in what seemed like seconds, carrying the pack he had filled earlier and another jacket similar to the one he wore.

"Put this on," he said, handing her the jacket.

When she had done so, he made sure once again that she could manage the pack. With a curt nod, he gestured toward the lake.

"They've cut the phone line and they've got the road blocked. We'll have to take another way out."

"We could cut through the woods."

"There are too many of them and they're spread out. We could walk straight in to a firefight."

She swallowed hard, but remained calm. He breathed a silent prayer of thanks for her courage.

"What about the lake?" she asked.

"Two problems. We don't have a key to the boat shed, and even if we did and we both could fit on the scull, I'm in no shape to row it."

"I could row."

"Not that scull. You'd never be able to keep it balanced, and if we went into the lake—" He shook his head. "It's fed by snowmelt. The water's still frigid."

"If we can't use the road or the woods or the lake, what does that leave us?"

John hesitated. He wished there was some alternative—almost anything—but try though he had, he couldn't think of one.

"The hills behind us. It's harder country than the woods, but we can cut through them and come out on the other side." He was about to continue when they both heard the sound of someone approaching. Actually, more than one someone. In the silence of the night, the movements of several people approaching up the road could be heard clearly.

Grabbing Lauren's hand, John headed around the back of the cabin. There was no time left. Billy and his boys would shoot at anything they saw move.

They reached the base of the hills and began climbing upward at the same time lights went on in the cabin.

Glancing back, they saw men beginning to search the outside.

"They know we're gone," John said. "My guess is they'll start by searching the woods."

"Then we'd better get moving."

Together, they began climbing the first hill. In daylight it would have been a pleasant excursion. In the dark with the temperature dropping and killers at their heels, it was anything but.

They climbed steadily for half an hour before Lauren said, "I've got to stop for a minute." She coughed, struggling to catch her breath and smiled apologetically. "I guess I'm not in as good shape as I should be."

"I was going too fast," John said. He looked back in the direction of the cabin. The lights were still on, but they were too far away to see where Panos and his men had gone.

Lauren took several deep breaths. She straightened the backpack. "I'm ready."

"We'll take it a little slower."

They resumed climbing. The next ridge was significantly higher than the first. Higher, too, than it had looked from the cabin. It was going to be a struggle getting over it.

Lauren stumbled once, catching her foot in the heavy undergrowth. John caught her before she could go down. "We'll be above the tree line soon," he said. "It'll get easier then."

He didn't add that once above the protection of the trees, they would be easier to spot by anyone with binoculars. Maybe it was just as well there were heavy clouds over the moon.

Something drifted past John's eyes. He barely noticed, but kept going. It happened again. Stopping, he looked up at the sky.

It was beginning to snow.

Chapter 17

"Snow," Lauren said. She held a hand out, catching a few stray flakes. "Look, it's snowing."

"I noticed." The grim set to John's mouth made it clear he wasn't reveling in this unexpected gift from nature.

"It's late in the year for this, isn't it?"

"Very. You okay?"

"Fine. You were right, it is getting easier."

They were almost through the trees. Ahead lay the crest of the hill. Lauren smiled slightly. Now that she was actually climbing it, she was more willing to call it a small mountain.

When this was all over, she was definitely going to get into some kind of exercise program. Any thought she'd had that racing around an emergency room every day was enough to keep her in good shape was fading rapidly. Her legs were beginning to ache and she could feel her heart pounding.

Of course, that just might have something to do with the men back at the cabin.

If they were still at the cabin. If they hadn't been smart enough to figure out where she and John had gone.

"Do you think Panos could follow us this way?" she asked.

"He's out of his element here. That's probably our best protection."

They continued climbing. Several minutes passed before Lauren spoke again. "You seem to know him pretty well."

"I think we were . . . associates."

"You mean you think you did what he does?" She couldn't hide her horror at the possibility even as she refused to believe it.

"No, not exactly." He shook his head. "I don't know. It's all fragments. There's a lot that doesn't make any sense. Maybe I don't want to remember."

"Because of what you think you were?"

He took her hand again to help her over a rock outcropping. The snow had begun to fall steadily.

"If you thought you were a drug dealer, responsible for spreading poison to millions of people, would you want to remember?"

"If I were capable of doing that kind of thing, I wouldn't care. I'd be without conscience. You aren't."

"So maybe getting shot made me a better person."

"That might play in a TV movie, but it doesn't happen in real life. Oh, I know people who come through near-death experiences swearing they're going to turn over a new leaf, but the fact is they stay pretty much the way they were. They don't go from being scum of the earth to Mr. Morality.''

He laughed. "Is that what you think I am?"

"I think you're a kind, decent man. I don't think you suddenly turned into that person because you got shot."

"Then what am I doing with two identities, a BMW, Savile Row suits, guns in my closet and acquaintances like Billy Panos?"

"Maybe you're a banker."

He turned and looked at her over his shoulder. "A what?"

"I'm serious. I've been thinking about it and you could be a banker. That would fit with the suits, the foreign travel, the car, all of it. Maybe you had these clients who seemed like okay people, but then you found out they were drug money and they turned on you before you could rat on them."

"My God, you've got an imagination."

"No, I'm serious. Why isn't that possible? You went to an Ivy League school, you were into crew, which is probably the most preppie sport going. You have very refined tastes in furnishings, cooking, books, everything. The fact is you practically shriek banker or maybe investment adviser, stockbroker, something like that."

"What about the guns?"

"Lots of people have them."

"Not the kind of assortment I've been keeping. At least, I hope not."

"Okay, the guns are a little hard to explain, but you've got to admit I could be right about the rest."

He sighed and, lifting her hand, touched his lips to it lightly. Snowflakes had caught on his eyelashes and on the lock of hair that fell across his forehead. He brushed them away, but they began accumulating again at once.

"I'm sorrier than I can say to have gotten you into this."

"So we'll get out of it. How many more of these hills can there be?"

"Several, but they're not the problem right now." He gestured at the sky. "We're going to have to find shelter."

"It's just a little snow. It'll probably stop soon." But even as she spoke, Lauren shivered. The flakes weren't the big, fluffy kind that looked so pretty. They had a fine, grainy texture she remembered from blizzards in the city.

And more were coming down with each passing moment.

By the time she and John crested the hill and entered the small ridge on the other side, the snow was falling so thickly that Lauren could barely see. She had to hold on to the back of his belt to keep on the track he cut for them both. Despite the layers of socks and boots, her feet were so cold that she could barely feel them.

She kept remembering the warning signs of frostbite. If they didn't find cover soon—

"There," John said. His voice was thick with relief. "I did remember it."

Lauren peered through the swirling snow in the direction he indicated. At first, she couldn't see anything but gradually, as they got closer, she made out a darker streak against the darkness of the hillside.

"What is that?"

"The entrance to a cave. It's right where I thought it would be. Apparently, I've hiked these hills before."

He must have to have led them so unerringly to what was probably the only shelter in miles. The cleft in the rock was narrow and easy to miss, especially in the midst of a snowstorm. They had to bend their heads to pass under the overhang.

Once on the other side, the change was startling. Instantly, the wind died and the stinging slap of icy flakes against their faces stopped.

John took a flashlight from the backpack and shone it around. The cave stretched far into darkness. Lauren could make out rough-hewn walls streaked with phosphorescent lichens, a ceiling from which stalactites hung and a floor that was smooth near the entrance but became more irregular as the cave went back. What surprised her the most were the colors. Everywhere the light shone, she saw vivid greens, yellows and purples, evidence of the different minerals that made up the rock and the various small-life forms that could grow on them.

"It's beautiful," she said softly, unwilling to disturb a silence that seemed almost reverent.

"Farther back a chamber opens up that's the size of a small stadium. There's also an underground river."

"How do you know that?"

"I've explored in here. Recently, I think. It may have been this past autumn. I remembered the trees outside. They looked almost as though they'd been on fire."

She rubbed her hands together, trying to revive the circulation in them. Despite the gloves she'd found in the jacket, her fingers were almost frozen stiff.

"I always promise myself I'll get out of the city to enjoy the foliage," she said. "But somehow it never works out."

"I know, it can be hard to get away. Sometimes you've just got to—" He stopped, staring off into the distance.

"What?"

He looked puzzled for a moment, then shook his head. "Nothing. Let's get settled in here. I'm going to try to find some wood that's still dry enough to burn. I'll be right back."

Lauren nodded, but her stomach tightened. The thought of being left alone in the cave while he ventured out into a blizzard scared her. But she kept quiet and busied herself by seeing what was in the backpack.

By the time John returned a short time later with an armload of wood, she was shaking her head over what she'd found.

"Forget banker. You're some sort of survivalist. Where did you get this stuff?" She gestured to the bedroll, small pots, packets of freeze-dried food, hunting knife, rope and various other items she'd discovered.

"Just the essentials if you're going to enjoy the wilderness," he said, shaking the snow off himself.

"How's it doing out there?"

"Getting worse. This is a full-fledged blizzard."

"That won't help Panos and his men."

"It should gain us some time," John agreed. He scooped out a small depression in the floor of the cave and began laying the fire. The wood was damp and took some effort to ignite, but finally flames caught. Lauren held out her hands toward them, grateful for the warmth.

She was exhausted. The adrenaline surge that had gotten her this far was fading fast. Her knees felt weak and she was beginning to shake all over.

John was beside her suddenly, a steely arm around her waist. His face was hard. "Sit down." He lowered her onto the bedroll near the fire. "You'll be better off if you get out of some of these wet clothes."

She was too tired to object or even dimly realize what he was doing. The full realization of how close they had come to disaster was sinking in.

"Don't think about it," he said as though reading her thoughts. Quickly, he stripped off the wet jacket and the sweater beneath. The fire leapt higher, casting a circle of warmth. He removed her boots and socks, rubbing her feet briskly to restore the circulation. When he was done, he wrapped her in a blanket.

"We need some hot food," he said.

She was so tired. With the return of warmth and the relative safety of the cave, it seemed as though all her strength had left her. Still, it wasn't fair that he should do everything. "I'll help." Her voice seemed to come from a great distance.

"No, you won't." He sounded gruff, almost angry. She sank back down on the bedroll, too worn out to argue.

The tiredness would pass. She would be back to normal any minute now. All she needed was a brief rest. Heck, she'd been through bad times in the ER when the crises seemed to come one on top of another. A little rest, something hot to drink, and she would be fine.

A while later, Lauren woke to the tantalizing smell of stew cooking. She sat up slowly and looked around in bewilderment.

The cave was real. She hadn't dreamt it. They were there, sheltering from the blizzard, and John was—

Sitting on his haunches in front of the fire, bare chested, the muscles of his back rippling slightly as he leaned forward to add another log to the flames.

Perhaps she was dreaming, after all. There was a rawly primitive beauty to the scene, disrupted only marginally by the gleam of an aluminum cooking pot.

She must have stirred or made some sound. He turned instantly, half rising. When he saw her sitting up, a slow smile curved his mouth.

"Feeling better?"

She nodded. "How long was I asleep?"

"About an hour. You needed it, but I'm glad you're awake. You really should eat."

She sniffed appreciatively. "What is it?"

"Beef stew. Dehydrated, of course, but edible. There's also some passable rice."

"You're amazing."

He looked surprised. "It's just basic stuff. Are you thirsty?"

"Yes, but if you pull a bottle of vintage burgundy out of that pack, I'm going to run screaming into the snow."

"Afraid not. You'll have to make do with coffee or tea."

They ate seated cross-legged on the bedroll. The stew was the best Lauren had ever tasted and she said so.

John laughed. "It's basic hiking rations—light to carry, easy to prepare and it won't actually kill you."

"That's more than can be said for the food at St. Mary's. How long do you think we'll have to stay here?"

The sudden change of subject didn't seem to bother him. "It's hard to say. My guess is the snow will end sometime in the next few hours. It's possible to get blizzards here that last a lot longer, but not at this time of year."

"Then we can walk out tomorrow?"

He hesitated. "I hope so, but it depends on how cold it is and how much snow is on the ground. It may be wiser for you to stay here while I go for help."

"No."

His brows drew together. "Just like that, no?"

"That's right. I found out what it feels like to wait for you before and I didn't like it."

"That was different. You're not anywhere near as strong as I am and you're not used to covering rough ground. You'll be safe here. I'll leave the food and—"

"No. I won't do it and the bottom line is that you can't make me. What if you fell? You could lie out there in the freezing cold with no one to help you. Besides, I may not be as strong, but I've got plenty of stamina."

"And courage," he said quietly.

She looked away self-consciously. "I don't know about that."

"I do. All right, we stay together."

"What made you change your mind?"

He smiled. "Didn't you say I couldn't make you?" The look he ran over her slender body made her flush. They both knew perfectly well that he could compel her to do anything he chose. Just as they both knew he would never take advantage of his strength.

"No, really, why give in?"

He took a swallow of the coffee. "Because it occurred to me that there's a chance, however slim, that Panos could follow us this far."

Lauren had a sudden, wrenching image of herself alone in the cave, confronted by the killer. "I see—"

"Don't think about it. For sure, he's not going anywhere tonight."

She nodded, suddenly grateful for the act of nature that might have meant the end for them both, but instead was providing them with the best protection they could hope for.

Her eyes met his. Softly, she said, "Neither are we."

He set the coffee cup down. His hand touched her hair, the curve of her cheek, the back of her head. Slowly, he drew her to him.

Chapter 18

He wanted to be slow and gentle, to give her all the care and patience this brave, beautiful woman deserved. But the gap between his intentions and his needs was a roaring chasm.

The mere touch of her skin against his had brought him fully, almost painfully erect. Even as a part of his mind marveled at his response to her, he could feel reason slipping beyond him. He took a deep, ragged breath, fighting the red mist that seemed to be moving through his brain.

In the shadows cast by the fire, she looked like a woman from another age, her hair tumbling down around her face, her eyes wide and watchful, assessing this male beside her. There was a stillness in her, a sense of waiting. She made no effort to pull away, but neither did she take the initiative.

They had made love already, he reminded himself.
They were lovers. He knew her body, or at least he was
beginning to, and she knew his.

But that had been in the cabin, in a bed, in that
world they had both occupied all their lives and where
they belonged.

This was different. Hidden away in the cave, shel-
tered from the blizzard, it was as though that world no
longer existed. They might have slipped back in time to
a vastly more primitive age where different rules ap-
plied.

A world in which a man might take a woman simply
because it suited him to do so.

He shook the thought away, surprised that it had
even occurred to him. He wasn't some sort of savage to
possess a woman without thought to her feelings or
wishes. The very idea of such behavior was repulsive to
him.

And yet he couldn't deny that she unleashed in him
a primal instinct to possess. He had felt it in the cabin,
though tempered by gentleness and the bonds of civilization. Both were now in danger of being forgotten.

He wanted her. All of her, in every way, for all time.
He wanted to brand her as his own so that no one—not
Lauren or he himself or anyone else—would ever for-
get it.

Death had come perilously close to taking her from
him. He was driven to fill her with life, a virile, purely
masculine challenge to the darkness lingering just beyond the light.

A tremor ran through him. He cupped the back of
her head, holding her in place for him, and took her

mouth. His kiss was thorough and demanding. He offered her no quarter, tasting and taking until he felt her unmistakable response. Her hands tangled in his hair as her hips moved seductively against his arousal.

He made a sound deep in his throat and pressed her back onto the bedroll. "You're wearing too many damn clothes," he said harshly and pulled a sweater off over her head. Underneath she wore one of his flannel shirts. He yanked the fabric out of the waistband and slid his hands beneath. Her bra had a front clasp. When it was opened, her breasts spilled into his palms.

He groaned, rubbing his thumbs over her distended nipples. She whispered his name against his throat and tugged at his shirt.

It was very warm in the cave, or perhaps the heat was in them. They undressed each other quickly, releasing buttons, lowering zippers. Firelight danced over their bodies.

She was paler than him and so finely, even delicately made that she seemed far too delicate a vessel for the strength he knew she possessed. By contrast, his body was darker, bronzed by the flames, corded with muscle and sinew.

"Let me," she whispered as she slipped his last garment from him. Her hands traced a path down his back, over his buttocks. When his sex sprang free, she made a small, gratified sound. The tip of her tongue moistened her lips.

"You are the most beautiful man."

He laughed, amused by the word she chose. But the sight of her naked, kneeling on the bedroll in front of him, made the breath catch in his throat.

He twisted his fingers in her feathery hair but said nothing, did nothing. She smiled against his skin. Her tongue licked a fiery path down his chest, lapping around his navel, moving lower.

He cried out once, hoarsely. The pleasure was so intense that his head fell back, his eyes closing against the wave after wave of sensation coursing through him. Scant moments passed before he knew he couldn't bear to wait any longer.

Swiftly, he drew her away and down, taking her beneath him, his sinewy thigh pushing hers apart. "Sweet heaven," he murmured against her mouth, "you're more than I ever dreamed. I can't get enough of you."

"Try," she whispered. "Please try."

Her husky plea shattered any remaining hope of restraint. He stroked the soft down of curls over her womanhood, his fingers probing her, confirming that she was ready for him. When he found her hot and wet, he almost groaned with relief. Opening her farther, he slipped the tip of his arousal into her.

It wasn't enough for either of them, but the sensation was enthralling. She clutched his back, her fingers digging into him, and raised her hips.

He moved a little farther, then thrust suddenly, hard and deep, burying himself in her silken sheath. For a moment he rested within her, his jaws clenched, before slowly, deliberately withdrawing almost completely.

She moaned in protest and wrapped her slender legs around him. "More . . . I want all of you."

He raised himself, bracing his weight on his arms, and gazed into her flushed face. So beautiful. What kind of man would he be if he didn't oblige the lady?

He did, repeatedly and extremely well, until her head was tossing back and forth and a high, keening moan broke from her. For a moment, he feared he might have hurt her, but she smiled through the mist of her pleasure and touched a hand lightly, reassuringly, to his mouth.

"What you do to me—" she began, only to stop as the tremors of release strengthened, passing through her like a hard, powerful current, drawing him with it.

They lay in a tangle of arms and legs, bodies glistening, until finally John stirred. The fire was dying down. Cool air brushed against them.

He drew a blanket over Lauren and got up to add more wood to the fire. She watched, her head propped against one hand. He was a magnificent sight, naked in the firelight, his body tall and powerful, capable of ruthless force and immense tenderness.

His back was perfectly sculpted, indented along the spinal column, tapering at his waist and hips. His buttocks were hard with muscle as were his thighs and lower legs.

He straightened and turned slightly, catching her eye. A teasing smile curved his mouth. "Enjoying the view?"

"Yes," she said unabashedly. "But I'd enjoy it more closer up."

He looked startled. "Why aren't you asleep?"

"Because I'm not." She sat up and deliberately let the blanket slip below her breasts.

He sighed. "I think I'm in trouble."

"Really?"

She moved, just enough to slide the blanket lower so that it barely grazed her hips.

"Scratch that. I'm definitely in trouble."

"Oh, well, if you're too tired—"

"Tired? You think because I got up in the middle of the night, tracked down a bunch of killers, hiked through a blizzard and made passionate love to you that I'm *tired?*"

"Don't forget making dinner."

"Right, thanks. And made dinner."

She pouted, marveled that she could do such a thing and sighed. "I'm being selfish. Forgive me?"

"I don't know—"

"I'm really sorry."

"You don't sound all that contrite to me."

"Perhaps I could find a way to convince you."

At least part of him seemed to find the suggestion interesting. Lauren laughed. She had a heady sense of freedom, as though all things were allowed.

"Nature's very unfair to men," John said, though he didn't seem to mind all that much.

"Actually, I'd say nature's been real good to you."

His eyes widened at her boldness. A moment later he grinned. "Why thank you, Ms. Walters."

"Oh, please, make it Lauren."

"You don't think that would be overly familiar?"

She laughed, enjoying the game. "We're very informal here."

He glanced at her naked torso, his eyes raking her breasts and the deep curve of her waist. "I can see that."

"We don't stand on ceremony."

"You're not standing at all."

"Good point. Why don't you come sit by me?"

"I suppose I could." He walked toward her, his body lithe and hard, his movement graceful. She took a deep breath, filling her lungs with the scent of the wood fire, the woolen blanket and beyond the snow-filled night.

When he was close enough, she reached up and took his hand, drawing him to her. He knelt close to her on the bedroll, not touching except where their fingers entwined.

"I owe you an apology," he said.

She frowned slightly, not wanting to hear him say again that he was sorry for what he had involved her in. The plain truth was that she wasn't sorry at all. He made her feel more alive than she ever had and nothing could make her regret that. Not ever.

But instead, he merely raised their joined hands and lightly brushed the small red spot on the upper curve of her breast. "It seems I was too rough." Quietly, he said, "I'm sorry."

He meant it. She could see the remorse in his eyes. Her throat thickened. "It's nothing."

"Oh, but it is. I'd like an opportunity to make it up to you."

She swallowed with some difficulty. There was a real question in her mind if she could survive that.

"It isn't necessary—"

"I insist." He took her other hand in his and slowly lowered her onto the bedroll. Smiling, he stretched her arms up above her head. Holding her like that, he lowered himself onto her.

Dimly, she realized that he wasn't letting her feel his full weight, but the sheer power of him was enough to make her tremble. She felt utterly helpless. What had begun as a game was suddenly very serious.

"Lie still," he said. Holding both her wrists in one hand, he began to move the other over her lightly, almost teasingly but with unmistakable intent. The pads of his fingers brushed down her throat, over the swell of her breasts and along the undersides. He refrained from touching her nipples, but merely circled them once, twice.

She moaned feverishly and tried to break free of his hold.

"You have to lie still," he said matter-of-factly, as though they were discussing what to have for lunch. His leg moved over hers, pinning her in place.

His hand moved along the curve of her waist, over her hips. It rested softly for a moment on her flat belly before lowering. His fingers parted her delicately, stroking the moist folds, probing gently.

"So beautiful," he murmured, his voice thick. He pushed her legs farther apart, positioning himself between them. His mouth teased hers, tasting, tempting. She arched her back, her breasts rubbing against the dusting of dark hair across his powerful chest.

He released her wrists, drawing her arms down and around him. "Hold me," he whispered as he took her nipple into his mouth, laving it with his tongue before suckling her urgently.

At the same time, he penetrated, sheathing himself inch by inch until he filled her completely, withdrawing, returning. He raised his head far enough to watch her, enthralled by her response. She was so innately sensual, so utterly giving, this enchanting woman he had somehow had the great good fortune to find.

The sight of her rapture was the catalyst for his own. He gathered her closer, holding her against all the world, and poured himself into her.

Chapter 19

Lauren woke first. She sat up and looked around the cave. Memory returned slowly and with it a sense of disbelief. It really hadn't been a dream? They actually had found shelter from the storm and—

Her hand went to her mouth, touching lips still slightly swollen from the passion of their lovemaking. She made a small sound. Next to her, John stirred slightly. He was lying on his side, facing her. Dark lashes fanned his cheeks. His lips were slightly parted. The hard lines of his face were relaxed. He looked younger, not quite so indomitable, but still devastatingly masculine.

Her gaze slid down his body. The blanket had slipped below his waist. In the dim light filling the cave, every plane and muscle seemed cast into relief. She might have been looking at a statue representing the

epitome of virility, save that no statue moved slowly
and rhythmically to life's breath.

In response, helplessly, her own body stirred. She
shut her eyes for a moment, fighting waves of hot,
languid desire. Truly, where he was concerned, satis-
faction was a remote conception. No matter how intense the fulfillment he drove her to, it merely left her
wanting—needing—more.

He made her feel insatiable, hungering, intensely
vulnerable and utterly shameless. He shook her entire
sense of who she was to the very core and left it, if not
in ruins, at least in danger of crumbling.

She'd always been wary of intimacy of all kinds, the
legacy no doubt of her turbulent upbringing. Sex had
struck her as overrated, not really worth the trouble
except for those lucky souls who seemed to believe in
love and actually find it.

Which meant—what? Sex with this man was the
primal force of life roaring through the universe. Intimacy seemed inevitable. She couldn't escape it if she
tried. Which brought her to love?

She shook her head stubbornly. Love was the deepest and most terrifying chasm in the landscape of life.
She had no desire to stumble into it. The problem was
it seemed that she already had.

Staring at him, as she might have a dangerous crea-
ture she had believed to be mythical, she bit down on
her lower lip. The small degree of pain helped drag her
from her wayward thoughts. Whatever her feelings
might—or might not—be, there was another reality to
deal with.

The storm appeared to be over.

Rising, she dressed quickly and went to the entrance of the cave. After hours in shadow, the daylight was almost blinding. She put a hand to her eyes and looked out onto a world transformed.

Soft, life-stirring spring was gone. In its place was diamond-white winter, hard edged, unyielding, dazzling. She breathed in deeply, inhaling ice-tinged air, and let the sun bathe her face. The sky was cloudless and the wind, which during the night had whipped the snow into drifts several feet high, had diminished to a murmur.

She took a step away from the cave and sank almost to her knees. But when she moved forward a few yards, the snow thinned so that she could walk comfortably. With a little practice, she could tell where the drifts were. If they could avoid them, they might be able to hike out without too much difficulty.

Lauren was turning back to the cave, intending to wake John, when a sudden sound from within brought her running. She gasped when she saw him. He was on his knees near the dying fire, bent over with his head in his hands. A low groan came from him.

Quickly, she knelt beside him. Her hand touched his shoulder. "What is it?"

He didn't answer at first and she wondered if he had heard her. His body rocked back and forth, mute evidence of a man in incredible pain.

"My head," he gasped. "I've never felt anything like this." He groaned again.

With a conscious effort, Lauren ignored the panic rising within her. She forced herself to think calmly and clearly. His skin beneath her hand was clammy. De-

spite the cool air in the cave, he was sweating pro-
fusely. What she could see of his features were
contorted in agony.

"You've got to lie down," she said and put an arm
around him, gently urging him back onto the bedroll.

The effort cost him dearly, but he complied. He even
managed to open his eyes and look at her.

"What's happening to me?"

"I don't know," she said, wishing with all her
strength that she did. The nurse in her could quickly
compile a list of possible causes, all of them unpleasant. But for the woman to confront what might be
happening to him—

He could be having a stroke. As young as he was and
as fit, that was a possibility in the aftermath of the serious injuries he had suffered. The odds were slim, but
just enough to terrify her.

There could also have been a head injury that somehow went undetected, but might explain his amnesia.
She had tremendous faith in the medical staff at St.
Mary's, but even they could miss something occasionally.

An extremely unusual adverse reaction to medications he'd been given could be causing him to hemor-
rhage. If so, there was no telling how serious that could
be.

The situation would be hard enough to deal with if
she had all the facilities of a topflight medical center.
Alone in the back of nowhere with nothing but a standard issue first-aid kit, she was virtually helpless.

All she could do was stay with him, holding on tightly to both his hands, and pray that whatever was happening would stop soon.

Long minutes passed. Without letting go of him, Lauren managed to reach the water they'd kept in a cooking pot. She soaked a handkerchief and used it to gently wash his face. He sighed faintly and closed his eyes, but his features did not relax. He was still in acute pain. Cursing her inability to do more, she crouched beside him, murmuring meaningless words of comfort and reassurance.

Finally, what seemed like an eternity later, his grip on her hands lessened. He slipped into sleep. Or unconsciousness. She was hard-pressed to know which. His breathing was regular and his heartbeat steady. Only partly reassured by that, Lauren continued to hold him.

Outside, the rising sun began to shine directly on the entrance to the cave. The greater light enabled her to see John more clearly. The hard lines of his face had eased somewhat. She pulled the blanket more fully over him and waited.

An hour passed, perhaps more. He moaned once or twice and several times appeared agitated. Kneeling as she was, Lauren's legs first became stiff, then numb. She was hardly aware of her own discomfort. It was inconsequential compared to whatever was happening to him.

Finally, just as she was beginning to think that she should get up and check to make sure there was no sign of anyone approaching the cave, John stirred. His eyes opened and he looked directly at her.

"Lauren."

It wasn't a question. He said it as though confirming that she was there.

She swallowed hard, struggling to conceal the wave of relief that threatened to swamp her. "How are you feeling?"

He didn't answer at once, but sat up and glanced around the cave, as though confirming his surroundings, too. His gaze returned to her. A faint smile lifted the corners of his mouth. "I'm usually more fun than this, really."

"You don't have to apologize. After what you've been through, it's only natural that—" She broke off, staring at him. The truth was there in his eyes, in his stillness as he waited for her to come to terms with it.

"You remember."

He nodded. "It felt as though my head was splitting open, but it was worth it."

Without warning, he stood. The blanket fell away. He stretched, luxuriantly naked, power flowing through him.

She watched, hardly breathing, dreading what he might say. Hoping. He picked up his clothes suddenly, dressed, ran a hand through his rumpled hair and reached for the guns he had been carrying. Swiftly, he checked each.

Only then did he come to stand in front of her, clothed and armed. His hands reached for her. Instinctively, he put her own in his and stood.

He drew her close against him, holding her as though she was made of porcelain. His chin brushed the top of her head. Quietly, he said, "I'm a narc."

She wasn't surprised. It fit perfectly. Moreover, it meant that her faith in him was vindicated. She shut her eyes for a moment in relief even as the full realization of the danger he faced swept over her.

"That's why Panos tried to kill you."

He released her from his hold, but only far enough so that he could look into her face. "You believed in me all along."

She shrugged. "I trust my instincts."

"If you'd been wrong—"

"I wasn't. Now about Panos, what are we going to do?"

"We're going to get out of here. I've got enough information to put him and a whole lot of other people away until hell freezes over, but it's not going to do any good unless it reaches the right hands."

"The weather's cleared. There's a lot of snow, but I think we can make it through all right."

"You understand we won't be able to hide our tracks?"

She nodded. He didn't have to tell her how very dangerous the situation was. They would be out in the open with nothing to hide them against the stark white of the landscape. And they would be slowed by the heavy snow. If they were spotted, they would stand a very good chance of being killed.

To die when there was so much yet to say and to know?

The thought twisted through her. She slid the straps of the backpack over her arms, took a deep breath and smiled.

"Let's get going."

Chapter 20

He had himself back. Having lived even a short time as a stranger within his own mind and body, John suspected he would never take the simple knowledge of himself for granted again.

Which was all well and good, and might provide some interesting philosophical speculation at another time. Right now he had only one thing to concentrate on—getting Lauren and himself out of the hills alive.

It was hard going. For all her courage and determined cheerfulness, he kept glancing at her with concern. Wading through several feet of snow was tough enough for him. He worried that she would become exhausted quickly.

The wind had died down and their clothes were adequate to keep them warm, except where they were buried in snow. Their pant legs would become wet, then soaked. Once that happened, frostbite would be a real possibility.

He stopped, looking out over a landscape beautiful in its grandeur yet undeniably dangerous. If they'd had skis or even snowshoes, it would have been different. But in the race to get away the previous night, he had not seriously considered that there might be a major snowfall. A few inches, certainly, but not this.

Lauren came up behind him. He had been cutting a trail for them both for more than an hour. Her hand touched his shoulder gently. "Are you all right?"

He looked down into her face, into the wide, luminous eyes, into the soul of this woman who had become all-important to him.

And he smiled.

"Never better. How are you holding up?"

"Fine," she said, as though that was obvious. "It's a magnificent day."

His surprise must have been evident. She laughed. "Well, you have to admit that it is. I know I'm just an ignorant city girl, but this is really spectacular. Besides, you're better and that has to count."

He looked away briefly, more moved by her words than he wanted her to see. Emotion wasn't his strong point. He'd spent too many years controlling and concealing it. Now that no longer seemed possible.

"I'd like to bring you back here," he said. "Under more, shall we say, conventional circumstances?"

Something flitted behind her eyes, wistfulness perhaps. It was gone so quickly he couldn't be sure.

"Have you come here often?" she asked.

He nodded. "I bought the cabin two years ago. Since then, I've used it as much as I could."

They began walking again.

"I knew I'd be working undercover, possibly for a long time," he went on, "and I needed a place to get away."

"It's been two years?"

"Just about. It took that long to set up the Santos identity, bring myself to the attention of the drug ring and eventually be accepted into it."

"What's your role supposedly?"

"Intelligence. I've provided information that's allowed the ring's couriers to avoid capture."

"You mean so drugs could get through?" The idea clearly disturbed her.

"That's what it took to win the trust of the ring's leaders and get me into their highest echelons where I'd be able to gather evidence against them. Believe me, I didn't like it, but there was no other way. The stakes were too high."

"It must have been extremely dangerous."

He shrugged. "Let's just say I was highly motivated."

"Because of your brother?"

He stopped, surprised, and looked at her over his shoulder. "How did you know that?"

"It was just a guess. We see so many people stabbed or shot in fights over drugs."

"Robbie wasn't doing drugs. He was as straight arrow as they come."

"What happened?"

He sighed. The memory hurt deeply, but it was his own and he was glad to have it, painful or not.

"We lived in Brooklyn, in a town house in a nice neighborhood. My dad ran an import-export business. Mom stayed home and looked after us."

"Were your father's ties to South America?"

John nodded. "His family was Venezuelan. He grew up there and in the States." A smile tugged at his mouth. "Mom was from Boston. It was an interesting match."

She stared at him, wide-eyed, amazed that her half-playful speculation had turned out to be so close to the truth. "So that's where Santos and Putnam came from?"

"My name, by the way, is John Putnam Santos. I went to Princeton, then Yale, became a lawyer and helped expand the business Dad founded. We did well."

He was being modest. They had done spectacularly, hence the Savile Row suits, the BMW, the picturesque but luxurious cabin. He'd had a privileged upbringing unmarred by the cruelty of the world—until Robbie.

"Robbie was my older brother. I'm only being honest when I say he was the best of us. I've never met anyone who cared more about other people. When the drug dealers showed up at our high school, Robbie didn't hesitate. He turned them in."

"They killed him?"

After all the years, it still hurt like hell. "They made bail and were back on the street within a couple of hours. My parents and Robbie weren't even told. My father was worried. He stood by Robbie's decision, of course, but he wanted protection for him. The police and the DA swore—I mean they absolutely swore—that his identity would be concealed, that our house would be guarded, Robbie would be watched. It was all lies."

"The authorities did nothing?"

"Zero. Later they claimed it was all a matter of confusion, the right orders not getting through to the right people. But that was bull. Drug money flows everywhere, corrupts everything."

"What did your family do?"

"We sold the house in Brooklyn, moved to the suburbs, tried to get on with our lives. We even managed it to a certain extent. But in the years since Robbie's death, the drugs have only spread further, reached deeper. The power of the drug cartels is so great now that they're essentially an enemy force that's invaded this country. The problem is that we've barely begun to come to terms with that and respond the way we need to."

"By going after the men who are really in charge?"

John nodded. "It doesn't do any good to target the small fish. They can be replaced so quickly the damage is never even felt. We need to put the overlords away. Instead of being the big men with the big money, they need to be breaking rocks for life with no chance of parole. Do that often enough and the most immoral, rapacious SOB will think twice about harming this country."

To achieve that, he had spent two years of his life living a lie. He had buried his own identity so deeply that it had almost slipped beyond his grasp. And he had come very close to dying.

"You got what you needed, didn't you?" Lauren asked.

"Finally. I know it all—names, account numbers, courier routes, everything." He touched a finger to his head. "It's all here."

"But they found out?"

He had a sudden, flashing image—himself in a plushly furnished office that could have belonged to a highly successful lawyer or investment banker, accessing a computer, reams of data flowing before his eyes, searching among it all for the core pieces of information he needed to finally put the puzzle together.

And then a sound off in the distance, startling him, the whir of an elevator.

"They caught me," he said simply. "I managed to get away, but not for long." He'd been heading back to his car when Panos closed in. Give the devil his due; he was good at what he did.

She stumbled. He turned quickly and caught her just as she would have fallen. Holding her close, he said, "I think we'd better rest."

"No, there's no time. We've got to keep moving."

Tears glinted in her eyes.

"You're hurt." Real fear coursed through him. He tightened his hold on her.

She shook her head and took a swipe at the glistening droplets slipping down her cheeks. "I'm just being silly."

No, not silly. Sad. This woman who had seen so much of the world's tragedy could still weep for him.

"Don't," he whispered, pleading, and touched his mouth to the salty fluid. "I'm going to win."

It was a promise to himself and to the woman who filled his heart and soul. But it was also a challenge hurled at capricious fate. He'd lost far too much, taken far too many risks, to believe in even the possibility of failure.

He would get them off this mountain. They would survive the storm, Panos, all of it. And then they would—

The thought, half-formed, dissolved. He looked up, into the crystal blue sky, unmarred save by a single black dot hurtling toward them.

Even as the telltale *whoop-whoop* of the copter's blades registered in his mind, he pushed Lauren down behind an outcropping and slipped the safety off his gun.

Chapter 21

Terror gripped Lauren. Pressed hard against snow-covered rock, she had to fight the urge to bolt. Squeezing her eyes shut, she told herself that whoever was in the helicopter might be trying to help them. It could be the forest rangers searching for hikers caught by the unexpected storm. Or it could be the police, maybe even the FBI. There was no reason necessarily to believe they were being hunted.

No reason, that is, until the first bullet ricocheted off the rock right near her face and disabused her of any thoughts of rescue.

"Panos," John murmured under his breath. He made the name sound like a curse.

Lauren swallowed against the bile rising in her throat. "What ingenuity. No wonder the guy's in demand."

"A regular go-getter." John pulled her farther down, his body covering hers. Bullets hit all around them. It was only a matter of time before the helicopter maneuvered in for a clear shot. He stuck his head up for a second, looking around. Wind had swept the snow from a narrow defile between two hills. If they could reach it, they might stand a chance.

He took Lauren's arm, pointing to the trail. "When I say go, you run for that. Keep low and move faster than you ever have in your life."

"What are you going to be doing?"

"Making Panos earn his money. Ready?"

"No, but I don't suppose that makes—"

He straightened just enough to aim. The automatic was a killing weapon. It had two full clips of ammunition attached, one at right angles to the other. The firing was in short, fierce bursts.

"Go!"

He had to trust that she obeyed. All his attention was on the copter. They had seen him, knew what he was doing and were veering hard to avoid his fire. The odds of hitting them were almost nil, but he had to try. If he could keep them off-balance long enough, Lauren would have a chance.

The copter steadied onto a new heading, coming directly at him. Whoever was flying, the guy had iron—

John dove over the outcropping, came up low and ran. Lauren was ahead of him, almost around to the other side. She would make it and he—

Rock splintered all around him. Close, very close. There was nowhere to go, nowhere left to hide. The defile was maybe ten yards ahead.

"Slide!" It was years ago, a summer day in Brooklyn, Little League ball, Robbie yelling to him from the sidelines as he brought the winning run home.

"Slide!" Not Robbie, Lauren. He threw himself flat, let the snow take him and slid, turning on his back, firing again. If they got him, he wasn't going alone.

Bullets struck the copter blades. The aircraft trembled. It was so close he could see the pilot and another man—Panos. Panos shouted something. The pilot yelled back, looking scared and angry as though he hadn't quite bargained on this, flying jock that he was but one not anxious to die.

The chopper veered off slightly, just long enough for them to reach the defile. John pushed Lauren in between the narrow walls of rock and followed her quickly. They were in a cleft rent between two sides of what was really the same small mountain. Sheer rock walls rose several hundred feet above them. There was barely enough space for two people to stand side by side. Sunlight filtered through, but only for the first few dozen yards. Beyond that lay darkness.

The sound of the chopper grew louder. It was returning for another pass. Grabbing Lauren, John pressed her between himself and the rock face. Bullets sprayed across the entrance to the defile, but it was so narrow that the chances of one actually entering were small.

"We're as safe here as we're going to get," he said. She was trembling slightly, but when she raised her face to his, her expression was calm.

"They'll run out of gas eventually, or ammunition."

He didn't say that long before that happened they would be looking for a place to land. Were, in all likelihood, looking already. Silently, he reviewed the terrain around the defile. The snow would disguise all irregularities in the landscape and make any attempt to set down treacherous. But for someone willing to take risks—paid to take them—perhaps even encouraged to take them by a man holding a gun to his head, all things were possible.

Besides, with Panos running the show, there was no guarantee that the chopper actually had to touch down. If it got close enough to the ground, he could jump.

There was no way up the sides of the defile. Even with rock-climbing equipment, the ascent would have been next to impossible. Emerging back into the open would only get them killed.

"We've got to move deeper," John said, "and hope this opens out somewhere."

"You didn't happen to ever explore this way, did you?"

"'Fraid not." He pulled a flashlight from his pack and shone it in front of them. Several dozen yards farther in, the defile narrowed even more. They had to continue single file with John in front. The chopper blades could still be heard, but they were muted, as though more distant.

"Could they be leaving?" Lauren asked.

"Nice thought, but I don't see why they would." He didn't add that it was more likely that the chopper had moved to the top of the rock face where the defile broke through to the sky. If Panos could reach there and position himself above them, they would be the closest thing to fish in a barrel that he was ever likely to come across.

Lauren said nothing more. He suspected she had figured out the situation for herself, and he was glad she didn't feel compelled to talk about it. They were moving at a pace as close to a run as they could manage through the defile. It continued to narrow, so much so that they had to slow down in order to squeeze through. Turned sideways, his face to the rock, John grimaced. "A few more servings of that duck and I wouldn't make it."

Several yards later, just when he thought they were at a dead end, the defile widened slightly. The chopper blades were louder, almost directly above them. Gunshots rang out, but John couldn't tell whether they were still coming from the chopper or if Panos had managed to get out.

Up ahead, a flash of daylight shone. The crack in the mountainside had led them all the way through and out the other end. John approached the opening carefully. A moment later, he saw that his caution was warranted. Whereas the opening on the other side was reachable by the trail, this one gave way to a sheer drop-off down the snow-covered mountain. He estimated that the terrain fell several hundred feet at a sixty or seventy degree angle.

Lauren peered over his shoulder. He felt her suck in her breath. "Oh, my God—"

Even as she spoke, the chopper swung around the side of the mountain and came directly at them. Panos was still aboard. They could see his face clearly. He looked madder than hell and out for blood. Theirs.

John stepped back quickly into the defile. He took the pack off, opened it and removed a waterproof sheet that he laid on the ground.

Lauren watched him, bewildered. "We're trapped. Whichever way we go, they'll be there waiting for us."

"And if we try to stay here, they'll put off men on the top and take us out that way."

Her eyes met his. For the first time, he saw real fear in her. "John—"

He stood and brushed the side of her face gently with his hand. "It's okay. Everything's going to be fine."

"How—?"

"You've gone sledding, right? Surely in the winter when you were a kid."

"Yes, but—"

"Think of this like that, only maybe a little bumpier. We're going to sit down on the ground cover." Suiting his actions to his words, he drew her with him so that he was positioned in front, facing the opening, with Lauren behind him. "Put your arms around my waist."

Realization dawned. He felt her stiffen. "You're kidding?"

"Got a better idea?"

"No, but—well, yes, actually I do. The way you're thinking, we're going to hit the slope from a dead stop. Stress on dead. It would be better if we hit it at a flat-out run."

His eyebrows rose. "And you thought I was kidding?"

"No, really, we can do it. Look, stand up."

He complied slowly, eyeing her all the while.

"If you hold the cover in front of you and we run, me right behind you, then you throw yourself flat just as we get to the opening, I follow and we go down the slope together much faster than we would otherwise. See?"

"You've been out in the cold too long. What are the odds you'll still be with me when I hit the opening?" The thought that he might lose her, that she might be left trapped and alone, stabbed through him.

"I'll be there," she said quietly. "Count on it."

He hesitated, but the look in her eyes said it all. In the final analysis, they had no choice.

"How fast can you run?" he asked.

She touched her lips gently to his. "Like a bat out of hell."

Not the description he would have chosen, but it reassured him nonetheless. They backed up farther into the defile. He shucked off the pack. It would only slow them down. One gun was put on safety and slung over his shoulder. He handed another to Lauren to do the same.

They were as ready as they were going to be.

John raised the cover sheet. It was just about his height. He held it so that he could see over the top.

"On three," he said.

She nodded against his back. Her hands gripped his belt.

"One...two...three..."

Like a bat out of hell. Like that summer day on the ball field. Like the hundred-yard dash that year in high school when he'd gone out for track and discovered he loved it.

He ran, straight down the narrow defile and out, hurtling into space. Time slowed. They seemed to hang suspended for a heartbeat. Then the white ground was rushing at them, coming at terrifying speed.

They landed hard, the breath knocked from them, saved from catastrophe by the softness of the snow. Gravity took the improvised sled, and they plummeted down the rock face.

Chapter 22

They were going to die.

The realization flashed through Lauren. She was living through the last moments of her life. This was it. Any curiosity she'd ever had about the time and means of her death was about to be satisfied forever.

Sorrow filled her. There was so much she'd left unsaid and undone, so much she would have liked a chance to do. All gone, vanished, in the blinding rush of speed and light that seemed to surround them like a tunnel. She couldn't breathe, couldn't see, couldn't do anything except hold on to John with all her strength and pray.

They hit something and careered wildly up into the air, slamming back down onto the improvised sled with such force that pain exploded in her. She would have screamed, but she had no breath. Her lungs were empty. The rush of adrenaline made her feel as though she were burning.

A tiny part of her mind seemed to stand apart, observing what was happening to them with almost clinical detachment. The ground gave way suddenly beneath them and they were airborne again, veering over to the right before landing again with another shock of pain.

She inhaled sharply, filling her starved lungs, and squeezed her eyes shut. A thousand fleeting impressions flashed through her mind—sunlit days, laughter and, above all, faces: family members, friends, patients she'd anguished over, people she hadn't seen in years in some cases, suddenly all drawn back through her mind in just a few seconds.

It was true, then, what people said, that you remembered your whole life. Would she soon know the truth about the rest—the rising out of the body, the beckoning light, all the things near-death survivors spoke of?

She didn't want to know, not for a long, long time. Damn it, she wanted to live. She wanted to laugh and love, to grow wiser and grow old, to hold a child of her own in her arms. To lose it all now was unbearable.

To die like this in the cold and the snow, hunted by evil men, filled her with rage.

Rage so all-encompassing that moments passed before she realized something had changed. They were slowing down.

The slope beneath them was no longer so steep. Hesitantly, she opened her eyes, catching a glimpse of trees, scattered at first, then suddenly thickening.

"Hold on!" John yelled.

He threw his weight to the left, knocking the sled over. Despite Lauren's best efforts, her grip on him was torn loose. She was thrown, rolling over and over, until she slammed into something freezing cold that billowed out all around her, swallowing her up.

White. Everything in the world was white. She couldn't see anything else. Frantically, she turned her head. The white was filled with light so intense that she winced. Was this it, then? Was she dead?

She inhaled, gasping. Dead people didn't do that, did they? Slowly, she reached out into the surrounding whiteness. Her hand broke free, into air.

And was grabbed.

Something immensely powerful and very fast hauled her upright. The white fell away. She saw trees, sky, the sun. And John's face, very close to her own as he held her with fierce strength.

"Lauren, thank God. When I couldn't find you—"

He broke off. She felt the tremor that raced through him and had to fight back her own tears. They had come so very close to death that life was suddenly, almost unbearably sweet.

But it was also far from assured.

"All in one piece?" he asked even as his hands moved over her, as though needing to reassure himself.

She managed a weak smile. "You?"

"Let's just say I don't think we discovered a new sport. Come on, let's move."

They climbed out of the snowdrift that had cushioned her fall and paused a moment to get their bearings. The forest surrounding them was so thick that Lauren was amazed they hadn't smashed into at least one tree. Through the thick trunks of pine, they could see the mountain rising up behind them. Ahead and to both sides, the ground continued to slope downward, but much more gently.

"This way," John said and headed almost directly to their left. "The trail we left will be visible from the chopper. Panos is likely to assume we'll go straight. If we keep to a zigzagging course, we've got at least a chance of evading him."

Lauren nodded. Even as John spoke, she became aware again of the sound of the chopper. It had never really gone away; she'd simply been too preoccupied to notice. But there was no doubt that they were still being hunted.

"How long do you think we can elude him?" Lauren asked.

"Until dark, I hope. Although there's a good chance they'll have to pull out to refuel before then."

She nodded. It would take luck, but they might be able to manage it. The question was, what then? They would be in the foothills with no equipment except their clothes and the guns. The snow had stopped, but it was still bitingly cold. She could feel it straight through to her bones.

John put an arm around her shoulders. He was no warmer than she, but the strength of his big, hard body comforted her.

"It's not as bad as it seems," he said. "I actually know where we are, or at least I've got a pretty good idea. There's a road about a mile north of here. Panos can see it from the air. He'll figure we're heading there and concentrate his efforts in that direction. So we go anywhere but and wait.''

"Then when he withdraws to refuel or it gets dark, we head for the road?''

John nodded. "Double-time.''

They moved on, holding each other. The going was tough. In the aftermath of their wild ride, as the adrenaline surge abated, Lauren felt exhausted. Only the constant sound of the chopper, now closer, now farther, kept her going.

"He's definitely concentrating toward the road,'' John said. They had paused for a few minutes to eat handfuls of snow. The icy liquid trickling down her throat revived Lauren somewhat, but she was well aware that her legs and arms felt like dead weights.

"How long has he been in the air, do you think?''

John shrugged. "It's hard to judge. The nearest airport is about an hour from here by car, probably only a few minutes by chopper. He could be up there quite a while yet.''

Lauren shaded her hands and stared at the dark, threatening shape veering back and forth across the sky. It looked like an ugly and very dangerous bird of prey.

She wrapped her arms around herself, shivering. "It's getting colder.''

"We'd better keep moving.''

They did, staying in the thick of the trees and as close to the ground as possible. Once the chopper veered in their direction. John flung Lauren to the ground and rolled with her into the long shadow cast by several trees. They lay there, trembling in the cold, as the chopper darted back and forth almost directly above them.

"Seems like Panos is losing patience," John murmured.

His breath was warm against her cheek, but the rest of her was freezing. She couldn't feel her feet at all. Everything she'd ever heard about frostbite told her they were getting very close to it.

"It would be better if we could find some shelter," she said.

"I know." His gaze swept over her. "But that isn't likely. Here, put your weight on me."

She laughed shakily. "That doesn't seem fair. Besides, your injuries—" Whatever color had been in her face faded. "Oh, my God, that plunge down the mountain— I didn't think—"

"I'm fine."

When she continued to look doubtful, he laughed. "No, really, there was no harm done. You should give your colleagues at St. Mary's more credit, not to mention yourself."

"I've got to admit, you must be one choice piece of stitching to hold up the way you are."

"Any truth to the rumor they use forty-pound line?"

Despite everything, Lauren grinned. She had a sudden, ludicrous image of Felix or one of the surgeons rigged out in a fishing vest and hat, tackle box at the ready, working on a patient.

"Strictly the best for our customers." She glanced up at the sky. The chopper had moved off toward the road. "We'd better keep moving."

They went on, plodding one leaden step after another. Much as she hated to, Lauren found herself leaning against John. She had very little strength left. Once, her knees buckled and she started to fall. Only the strength of his arm around her waist stopped her.

"We'd better rest for a while," he said, drawing her into the thick shadows between several trees.

She slid down onto the ground with a weary sigh, hardly feeling the cold anymore. John crouched beside her, holding her close. His embrace was strictly platonic but immensely comforting.

Lauren leaned her head against his chest. She was so tired she felt about ready to cry, but absolutely wouldn't let herself. That much, at least, she could still do.

"You know what my idea of paradise is?" she asked, hearing her own voice as though from a distance.

His arms tightened. "What?"

"No chopper blades."

She felt the soft rumble of a chuckle in his chest. "That'd be great. It would—"

He stopped. They looked at each other even as their exhausted senses realized what was missing.

"It's gone," Lauren said.

She looked up, following the direction of John's gaze. The sky was empty.

The tears did come then, even as she scrambled to her feet and he did the same.

"We're within a quarter mile of the road," John said. He looked at her with concern. "Can you make it?"

"Of course." She sounded far more confident than she felt, but then there really was no choice. If Panos had gone to refuel, he would be back. They didn't have a second to waste.

Luck was with them. As they neared the road, the snow cover thinned and the going got easier. Once Lauren could actually see the thin ribbon of light gray standing out against the white landscape, she felt a surge of strength.

"How far from here to town?" she asked.

"A couple of miles, but there's tree cover a good part of the way. We just have to get through this stretch."

He didn't have to explain. If the chopper returned while they were walking along the exposed road, they wouldn't have a chance.

"Maybe a car will come along," Lauren said and prayed it would be so. It was extraordinarily quiet. In the absence of the chopper, her city-trained ears could make out nothing but the vague sound of wind rippling through the pines. They seemed to be the only people on earth.

With every step requiring a maximum effort, Lauren had no inclination to talk. Her lungs burned. She knew they should be running and suspected that John was still capable of that. But she was not, and he had deliberately slowed his pace to the fastest she could match.

She was grateful, but at the same time deeply worried.

"Maybe we should split up?"

His head jerked in her direction. "What?"

"You go on ahead for help. I'll follow." When he continued to stare at her as though she must be crazy, she said, "You can go faster than this. We both know that."

"I don't care. We stay together."

"That's nuts and Panos is probably counting on it. He'll be saved the trouble of hunting two targets instead of one."

John made a sound of disgust deep in his throat. "He doesn't even know we're still alive. Odds are he figures we died going down the mountain."

"City boy," Lauren said and laughed. She actually laughed. Not very well, but it still counted. "Oh, God, I think I'm losing my mind."

"If you really believe I'd leave you, then you are."

Her hand tightened on his arm. "John, seriously, you don't believe he isn't coming back, if only to search for bodies? I mean, the people he works for, do they pay without evidence?"

"He'll tell them what we did. They'll believe we're dead."

"You didn't answer my question. He goes and tells these guys some cock-and-bull story and they just believe him and say okay, here's the money, have a nice day?"

"Probably not the nice day part."

"Yeah, right. He's coming back."

"Okay, so he is. I'm not leaving you. Look up ahead there, you see those trees?"

She did even though it was getting harder to see anything. The light was fading and, besides, she was so very tired. But there they were, a thick dark shadow into which the road seemed to disappear.

"It's not much farther," John said.

In fact, it was, but she was willing to be lied to just this once, by this man. They stumbled on. With taunting slowness, the trees inched closer.

Lauren was actually starting to believe they were going to reach them when off in the distance, faint but unmistakable, she heard the sound she knew would haunt her dreams forever. Presuming she ever dreamt again.

The chopper was back.

"Run!" Holding her, John sprinted for the trees. Lauren glanced back once over her shoulder. Two men were hanging out the sides of the chopper, both firing. Bullets flew all around them. A scream rose in her throat, but she had no air for it.

Splintered rock flew up from the surface of the road. A sharp piece struck her in the forehead, but Lauren hardly noticed. After all they had survived, all they had endured, it seemed grossly unfair that they might yet die.

Might? Sweet Lord, who was she fooling? They were out in the open, still a good hundred yards from the trees, and even if they did reach them, so what? It would be far easier for Panos and his men to simply spray the whole area with automatic arms fire. They would be wounded at the very least, if not killed outright.

And if they were merely wounded, they would lie there in the cold and the dark, waiting for the hunters to close in and finish the job.

And people thought the city was dangerous?

Absurdly, that was all she could think of as the bullets flew and the chopper roared and death inched ever closer. Just let her get back to New York and she would kiss the ground. No, really she would. A big smacker right on the sidewalk in front of St. Mary's. Okay, maybe she would pour a little antiseptic on it first, but what the hell, she would be back.

A bullet whizzed past her cheek. She felt the hot rush of blood down her scalp.

They fell. She had no idea exactly why, although exhaustion, hypothermia and getting shot probably had something to do with it. John twisted so that he was on top of her. She couldn't stand that, couldn't bear the thought that he would die like that, trying to shield her.

Goddamn them to hell and back, Panos and all the filth who cared nothing for anything or anyone. How dare they live? How dare they make it so hard for decent people to find a safe place in the world? If only—

The frantic rush of her thoughts shattered. She held on to John with all her might, thinking that maybe she'd been shot again, maybe her mind was playing some bizarre trick on her.

For at that moment, as the sun sank beneath the western hills and night descended on the bucolic Vermont country road where they lay, she could have sworn she heard a second chopper.

Coming hard and fast out of the east, a huge black stain against the sky, bigger by far than the chopper Panos and his men were in and sounding vastly more powerful.

A chopper that dove hard and fast straight toward the smaller aircraft. Over John's shoulder, she could see flashes of red coming from the bigger chopper. She heard a whoosh and saw something large, incredibly fast, burst from beneath the attacking vehicle.

"Holy—" John muttered. He never got the rest out. Panos and his men had guns, standard killing weapons of their kind. But they didn't have missiles. Whoever was in the other chopper did and had just launched one directly at them.

"Oh, my God—" Lauren breathed. She'd seen it happen on television and the movies, but never in her wildest dreams had she imagined she would witness it in person. The trail of the missile was clearly visible in the glare of light from the attacking chopper. They watched it millisecond by millisecond as it closed on its target.

Panos's pilot saw it, too. He tried desperately to evade the weapon, but there was no time. Lauren shut her eyes an instant before the impact. She heard but did not see it.

There was a roar, then another, the scream of metal and the sudden howl of fire springing to life. The sound was deafening, the heat scorching. Debris rained down on them.

Lauren had no clear memory of reaching the trees. When she was next aware, she was crouched next to John in the shelter of the woods, watching.

The other chopper had landed. Men got out. Big, hard men wearing jumpsuits and carrying automatic weapons. Several surrounded what was left of Panos's chopper. Another glanced in their direction, saw them and broke into a trot.

By the time he reached them, they were on their feet. The man looked at Lauren briefly, then turned his attention to John.

"This was fun, but maybe next time you could just call the office instead of making us run all over creation trying to find you?"

"Oh, I don't know," John said. "You desk jockeys got to get out some time."

He laughed. So did the other man. They then did one of those male things that seemed to involve both hitting and hugging each other.

"I'm glad you two are happy," Lauren muttered. She sat down in the snow. They could grin at each other all night for all she cared. She was just going to have a little rest. Then she would do something about her forehead and the feet she couldn't feel and getting back to civilization.

Just a little rest. Her head fell forward. She never heard John yell her name or saw the other men come running.

Chapter 23

It was brown and it had some kind of liquid poured over it. There was an orange thing next to it and a blob of what were probably mashed potatoes. Lauren poked the meat—she was being kind—with her fork but made no attempt to eat it. She wasn't hungry.

"Come on," Ginny Germaine said. She was on her break and had come up to see Lauren. Her smile should have been enough to pierce the gray cloud that seemed to have swallowed the day, but it barely got through.

"It's not that bad," Ginny said, although her expression as she eyed what was on the plate said otherwise. "Can I run out and get you a burger?"

Lauren pushed the tray table away. She had a room to herself with as decent a view as St. Mary's was ever going to be able to provide, good friends who kept dropping in to try to cheer her up and an excellent prognosis.

"Slight concussion," Felix had said as he checked the scalp laceration to make absolutely sure the Drug Enforcement Administration medic had taken care of it properly. "Takes more than a bullet to dent this hard head" was his professional opinion.

She would be fine.

Lauren shifted on the bed, trying to find a more comfortable position. "I shouldn't even be here."

"That's what all you patients say. Your chart says otherwise."

"I hate having a chart. The only chart I should have is somebody else's. A nurse has no business lying in a hospital bed."

"She does when she's been trudging around in below freezing temperatures, camping out in a blizzard and getting shot. Oh, yes, what's this I hear about some kind of wild sled ride down the side of a mountain?"

"Remind me not to take up the luge. Seriously, when am I getting out?"

"Not up to me," Ginny said, briskly patting her covers. She glanced at the rejected tray. "Try to eat something."

"I'd rather die."

"You had your chance. Now you gotta eat."

"Eat? Who's not eating?" Martha Morrissey popped her head in the door, saw Lauren and grinned. "Don't worry, I'm not here to ask you to work an extra shift."

"I'd take it if it would get me out of this bed."

"She would, too," Ginny said. "You've got to watch her."

Martha came over and gave Lauren a hug, careful not to squeeze too tightly. "So how are you doing?"

"I'm fine. I need to get out of here."

Ginny and Martha exchanged a glance. An unspoken message seemed to pass between them.

"Now, honey," Martha said gently. "You've been through a really rough time. It wouldn't do any harm for you to get a few days' rest."

"I can rest at my place."

"And miss all the pampering we dole out here," Ginny said, "not to mention our fine cuisine? How could you possibly pass that up?"

"I c-could manage...." Oh, God, she was going to cry. Her lower lip was trembling and she couldn't fight the all-over weepy feeling that had swooped up out of dead center of her psyche.

"Honey—" Ginny sat down on the side of the bed and put an arm around Lauren's shoulders.

Martha did the same. "It's okay, kid. Sometimes you've got to let it out."

"But it's so stupid," Lauren said. She swiped at the tears running down her cheeks. "I could have gotten killed and I'm crying about a couple of stupid ducks."

The two women looked at each other. "Ducks?" Ginny repeated.

"John cooked them w-with currant s-sauce...."

Out of the corner of her eye, Lauren saw Martha mouth a single word. "Litzer?"

"I don't need a neurologist. I'm not going crazy or I already am, either way there's nothing good Dr. Litzer can do for me." She sniffled loudly.

"John's a wonderful cook," she explained. "You wouldn't necessarily think it to look at him, but he really is."

"That's nice, honey," Ginny soothed. In an aside to Martha, she added, "That man's got a lot to answer for. He took the best damn nurse I ever saw and turned her into a weepy little thing getting all upset about dead ducks."

"I think there may be more to it than that," Martha said.

Ginny snorted. "No kidding? She's got it about as bad as I've ever seen. Question is, what's he gonna do about it?"

"John's the bravest man I've ever known," Lauren informed them. "He kept trying to protect me. I didn't want him to, but—"

"Cooks, does the Sir Galahad bit and looks like a Greek god." Martha sighed. "You're right. She's in big-time trouble."

"And we've got to help her. After all, what are friends for?"

"Good friends," Lauren said and looked at them both through her tears. "I never really told you that, did I? I mean, how much I care about you both? But now everything seems different. Have you ever really looked at a drop of rain on a flower? It's absolutely incredible, like a whole universe—"

"She's not high, is she?" Martha asked over her head.

"I don't think so, but maybe we ought to check her meds. This sure isn't our Lauren."

"I don't know what's wrong with me," Lauren interjected. "I don't seem to recognize myself anymore. I've turned into this stranger who wants to cry all the time and keeps thinking about—"

"Ducks?" Ginny offered. "Honey, you've been through a terrible experience. Now I don't have to tell you about what trauma like that does to a person, do I? You've got to expect to be a little fragile for a while, but you'll snap out of it."

"I don't know—"

"Sure you will," Martha said. "How about I run over to your place, get you some of your own things? They'll make you feel better."

Maybe they would. She sure wasn't going to feel any worse. Her emotions hadn't done somersaults like this since she was a teenager, and even then they'd behaved better.

"That would be nice. Thank you."

Martha and Ginny conferred outside her door for a few minutes. Martha headed off to her apartment, Ginny went elsewhere. Ginny returned first.

"They didn't have any duck," she said as she began unpacking the bag she'd brought from the deli across the street. "But I remembered you liked this, and it's a lot better for you than a burger and fries, not to mention what our esteemed cafeteria is dishing out."

Ginny unloaded several plastic containers, one containing pasta salad with broccoli, another with chicken soup and a third filled with rice pudding.

"Maybe not what the dietician would order, but definitely comfort food. Eat up."

"Thanks," Lauren said and sniffed again. Ginny really had brought her favorites, the things she got for herself on the truly bad days if she was lucky enough to grab a couple of minutes to run across the street. Once she'd eaten an entire pint of rice pudding sitting in the women's locker room, trying to forget a seventeen-year-old who had died an hour before from a stab wound.

"Smells delicious," she said, opening the chicken soup first.

"You eat all of it," Ginny admonished. "Then maybe you'd like to read a few magazines. I brought these." She plopped down a selection of the magazines best known for recipes, decorating tips and child-care columns.

"Uh, thanks," Lauren said, eyeing them. She'd never had time to read anything like that before, not to mention having had no particular inclination. But something about "cozy decorating for two" caught her notice and she thought she might just glance at it.

Besides, she didn't want to hurt Ginny's feelings. With that in mind she finished all the chicken soup before her friend left to go back on duty and was tackling the pasta salad when Felix popped in.

"Hey, kid, how's it going?" he asked with a grin.

"Let's just say I think we should all be forced to spend a couple of days viewing the world from this perspective."

Felix laughed, but he also looked her over in one, highly professional glance. "Still shaky, huh?"

"No, I'm not. I'm just tired. Do you have any idea how hard it is to get a decent night's sleep in this place? People are coming and going at all hours. I barely closed my eyes."

"Night shift says you slept fine."

"I was faking." She hadn't been, but the food was restoring her spirits. She didn't feel quite so limp anymore.

"Yeah, well, I just dropped around to tell you, there have been a whole bunch of arrests."

"Oh—" God help her, she couldn't sound even a little bit casual. Since arriving at St. Mary's the previous evening, she hadn't seen or heard from John. He'd been whisked off in a whirl of activity after hugging her fiercely hard, saying he would be back and kissing her so thoroughly that it was at least five minutes before she breathed again.

"They're calling it the most important counteroffensive against the drug kingpins that's ever happened. There have been at least a dozen arrests here in the States, all very high-level people, and more arrests in several other countries. Maybe more to the point, there have been seizures of hundreds of millions of dollars in offshore bank accounts and property. The consensus is that this might actually be a turning point."

"All because of one man—"

"Our Mr. Doe? The media doesn't seem to have anything on him. They're identifying him as an undercover operative who infiltrated the drug rings and worked for years winning the trust of the kingpins. He sounds like a combination of Superman and Dick Tracy."

"With maybe a little Julia Child."

"What?"

"Never mind. I'm just glad it all worked out." She was, really. John had the great success he'd sacrificed so much to achieve. He would be able to go back to the work he obviously loved. With his identity still hidden, he might even be able to continue working undercover. Who knew what he would infiltrate next? Gunrunners? Terrorists? Nuclear technology smugglers? The sky was the limit for a guy with his talents.

"Lauren—" Felix was bending over her, looking anxious.

"No, I'm fine, really. I just wish the world was different."

"Don't we all. Look, if there's anything I can get for you or do—"

"You can back your cute little butt out of this room and give our mutual friend some privacy," said Martha. She cast Felix a meaningful glance as she bustled in, bearing an overnight bag.

"I found everything, no trouble. Now if God's gift to medicine will find somewhere else to be—"

Felix raised his hands in surrender. "I'm outta here."

When the door had closed behind him, Martha grinned. She set the bag down on the bed. "Now don't get mad. I didn't bring exactly what you asked for. How can you lie around in some blue flannel nightshirt when you've got all that gorgeous lingerie hidden away? I thought this would be perfect—"

She pulled out a delicate ivory silk negligee trimmed in coffee-hued lace and a matching peignoir. "Honey, you've got great taste. I just love this stuff."

"So do I, but I don't think it really works here."

Martha was not discouraged. She laid the lovely garments on the bed and continued emptying the bag. "There's nothing better for your morale. Now you know how important a person's spirits are to getting better. You put all this pretty stuff on, fix your hair, maybe add a little makeup, and I guarantee it'll be the best thing for you."

When Lauren still hesitated, she put her hands on her hips and looked at her sternly. "Lauren Walters, I've seen you go to the mat for patients anyone else would have written off. You going to tell me you won't do this teeny-weeny little thing to make yourself feel better?"

"I'm liable to feel ridiculous, is all."

"And why would that be? You're not supposed to be beautiful and feminine? You're just supposed to be some workhorse? Honey, you're a woman. A smart, funny and not-too-hard to look at one. It's time you gave yourself that."

Lauren looked at the negligee and peignoir. She'd bought them for herself on a day when she needed some special cheering up. They made her feel as though she had a part in a world that was gentler and more filled with possibilities than the one she actually inhabited.

Or had inhabited before a certain John Doe showed up in it.

"All right," she said suddenly. Before she could change her mind, she slipped her legs over the side of the bed. "Nobody will believe it's me, but maybe that's all for the better."

By the time Martha left half an hour later, Lauren wasn't sure how she felt. The touch of silk against her skin was luxurious. The scent of her favorite perfume softened the medicinal edge of the hospital air. When she closed her eyes, she could almost pretend she was somewhere else.

The cabin, for instance. She could see the fire dancing and herself, in John's arms, the hard length of his body against her, his arms protection against the world.

Her eyes flew open. She couldn't stand the yearning her memories triggered. It was as though a deep, empty place opened inside her and threatened to suck her in.

Despite the warmth of the hospital room, she shivered. She was being ridiculous. This was where she belonged, not in the bed but certainly in St. Mary's. She would be back to work in another day or two. With the city's constant stream of casualties flowing through the ER, she wouldn't have time to feel sorry for herself.

Or wonder where John was, what he was doing. If he was all right.

There was a remote control for the TV beside the bed. Lauren hadn't bothered with it since being admitted, but now she switched on a channel at random. A hyperactive coyote ran smack into the side of a hill, digging out a coyote-shaped tunnel in the process.

Click.

Two very attractive people—one man, one woman— lay apparently naked, entwined on a bed, talking seriously about a mutual friend they believed might be suffering from multiple personality disorder. Or had possibly been reincarnated.

Click.

A woman jumped up and down, waving her arms and screaming over and over, "Twelve dollars and ninety cents."

Click.

"More on the major drug bust story we reported earlier. Federal officials are now saying that this is definitely the largest and most significant victory in the war against drugs." The silver-haired, tanned news anchor looked into the camera meaningfully. "Arrests now stand at twenty-one in the United States with an additional two dozen suspects detained outside the country. Highly placed sources say that total confiscated bank accounts and other holdings may exceed one billion dollars."

The elegant blond woman with the permanent smile who was co-anchor on this, one of America's most popular news shows, jumped suddenly as though she'd been stuck.

"Dave, did you say a billion?" Her expression suggested she thought good old Dave might be losing it.

Dave smiled tolerantly. "Yes, Jenny, incredible though it may sound, I did say billion with a *B*." His expression sobered. "I'm afraid that only confirms what we've all suspected for some time, namely that illegal drugs have become very big business."

No dust on good old Dave, Lauren thought. And no dust on John, either. Whatever the federal government paid him, he'd just made it back for them in spades.

"There's still no information on the identity of the undercover operative who broke the case, is there, Dave?"

"No, Jenny, I'm afraid not. Our good friends in Washington are playing this one very cool. Apparently, they intend for our unsung hero to stay that way."

"That's rather refreshing, don't you think, Dave? I mean, after all, we're living in this era of instant celebrity when it seems everyone's either a guest on a talk show or hosting one."

"Not us, Jenny. We're here, night after night, just doing our darnedest to keep the citizens of this great country informed. But I agree with you, there's something a bit nostalgic about having an unknown hero who rides to the rescue, sort of a masked man on a white horse—"

"Actually, Zorro rode a black horse, Dave."

"No, I was thinking of the Lone Ranger, Jenny. Now he rode a white horse."

Lauren groaned. She clicked off the TV and tossed the remote back onto the bedside table. No wonder John and his colleagues wanted him kept out of the public eye. You didn't reward a man who had given two years of his life and damn near died in the process by sending him out to cope with the media.

But how did you reward him? Where would John go from here? Once all the danger and excitement were past, what would he want?

And what would he regret?

They had come together under such extraordinary circumstances without any thought or restraint, two people for whom all the ordinary rules hadn't seemed to apply. But that was then and this was now. She had to face the fact that he might want to put what had happened between them in the past.

Her throat tightened. She had to concentrate very hard on not crying.

When the worst of the urge was past, she took a deep breath. "Don't be an idiot, Walters," she murmured. "You don't know anything about what the man thinks or feels."

She knew his passion and his courage, but not his heart. She would be a fool to pretend otherwise.

Besides, dealing with her own emotions was enough of a challenge without trying to imagine his.

Could she envision a future with a man who lived with profound danger as a matter of daily routine? She'd been at St. Mary's when police were brought in who had been shot. She'd seen the agony of their wives and children. She'd felt the horrible, tearing helplessness at losing good, valiant men.

How much worse it would be to actually love a man like that.

Lauren laid her head back against the pillows and closed her eyes. There were thousands of ways a man who put his life on the line for what he believed in could be killed. Unfortunately, she'd seen a good percentage of them over the years, enough to send her imagination into overdrive.

Her hands balled into fists against the covers. "Damn—"

"Maybe I should come back—"

Lauren's eyes shot open. A beautiful older woman was standing at the door to her room. The woman was elegantly dressed in what even Lauren could recognize had to be a designer suit. She had the kind of classic beauty built on bone structure and character that only improves with age.

And she was smiling, if rather uncertainly.

"You are Lauren Walters, aren't you?"

"Yes, I am, and you're—" An incredible possibility was stirring in Lauren's mind. The woman's eyes reminded her of—

"I'm Anne Santos, John's mother. He's terribly sorry that he's been tied up with work, and he asked if I'd come by and see to anything you might need." She came a little closer to the bed, looking at Lauren with concern but also interest. "He tells me you're a nurse."

Lauren nodded. John's mother. He'd sent his mother. How very nice. Just the person she wanted to meet today.

"Yes, I am. I work here at St. Mary's. Won't you sit down?"

"Thank you. If you don't mind company, I believe I'll stay awhile. John was very rushed and didn't have time to tell me much, but I gather the two of you had a rather incredible adventure."

Lauren thought of the flight from Panos, the ride down the mountain, getting shot at from the chopper, thinking she was going to die, not to mention what had gone on before all that. Definitely not to mention. Mrs.

Santos looked like a lovely woman. There was no reason for her to hear all the details.

And a good many reasons why she shouldn't.

"It certainly was. I'd never been to Vermont before. It's very picturesque."

Mrs. Santos looked at her a little oddly. Her mouth quirked. "It certainly is. Are you from New York originally?"

"The Midwest, but I've lived in New York quite a few years now."

Oh, God, she was at a tea party. Any minute, the Mad Hatter would show up.

"Your work must be very demanding. I understand you were on duty the night John was shot."

For a guy who hadn't had time to say much, he hadn't done too badly.

"I'm an ER nurse. John was badly wounded, but he's made a terrific recovery."

Actually, an astounding one given what she could say personally about his stamina. Very personally.

A look of pain passed over Anne Santos's face. "I was in Europe so I didn't see the news, and John's brothers are scattered all over the country so they didn't, either. Apparently his colleagues were used to him being out of touch. Even so, of course they recognized him from the news reports. I gather there was some debate over what had actually happened, whether his cover had been...blown, I believe the word is? But they were about to come in here after him when he—"

"Left?"

Anne gave her a grateful look. "Yes, left. Is it true he had lost his memory?"

Lauren nodded. "Classic post-trauma amnesia, although I think in John's case some of the difficulty may have come from how deeply he had buried his own identity in order to work undercover."

"My husband thought that might be the case. By the way, Carlos is looking forward to meeting you."

At a loss as to what to say, Lauren fell back on a smile. Anne Santos was a genuinely nice woman. Not for the world would Lauren want to hurt her. But it seemed as though she was presuming a lot.

"That's very kind of you. I also really appreciate your coming, but I wouldn't want to put you to any trouble."

The older woman looked amused. "Oh, I assure you, it's no trouble at all. You have no idea how long Carlos and I—" She stopped abruptly and cleared her throat. "Forgive me. We've been so worried about John that I haven't been sleeping. When I get like this, I tend to rattle on."

"So do I," Lauren said. "There's nothing like a week of double shifts to loosen my tongue."

"Do you have to do that very often?"

"The hospital's short staffed. Everyone's putting in overtime."

"That must be very hard on you."

"It's made me question the job," Lauren admitted. She could hardly believe she was saying that to a woman who should have been a total stranger but who somehow didn't seem that way. "Actually, I'd been questioning it for a while. I just couldn't seem to envision doing anything else."

"My husband was like that for years. He built a very successful business and made a real difference in many people's lives. But once that was accomplished, the daily grind began to wear him down. Fortunately, he's been able to turn over day-to-day operations to two of our sons. The past few years we've been traveling."

"That was why you were in Europe?"

Anne nodded. "The south of France. It was marvelous. We went to this little village off the beaten track and—"

Laughter. Out of breath, in a tearing hurry, John came around the corner of the hospital ward and skidded to a halt. His coat flapped open, his hair was rumpled and he was clutching a bouquet of roses. A passing orderly grinned at him.

He barely noticed. Without sleep for two days, unshaven, his last meal consisting of barbecue-flavored nachos from a vending machine eight hours before, he was surrounded by a pleasant sense of unreality.

Until he heard the laughter. Very belatedly, his exhausted brain signaled that maybe he should have thought twice about asking his mom to drop by and keep Lauren company. But he'd felt so badly about not being able to be there with her himself.

They sure did seem to have hit it off. As he neared the door, he heard Lauren say, "No, he didn't? What happened then?"

"Oh, well," his mother replied, "there was nothing to do except call the fire department. They came right away and were very good about it, but it was years before he could look at a goat again."

Oh, no, not the story about him getting his head caught in the wrought-iron fence at his grandparents' farm in Massachusetts and the neighbor's goat coming over to chew on his hair. If she was down to that one, there was no telling what would come out of her mouth next.

"Of course, that wasn't anywhere as bad as the summer we absolutely could not get him to wear clothes. He was three then and he just couldn't see the point."

"It could have been worse. He could have been sixteen."

"By the time he reached that age, I made it a point not to inquire too closely. But seriously, John has always been the most considerate of sons. You can tell a great deal about a man by his feelings for his parents and—"

"Mom," John interrupted, more or less throwing himself into the room. "It's great that you got here. How are you doing?" Before she could answer, he gave her a quick hug that robbed her of breath momentarily. That might be the desired effect, Lauren thought, even as he turned his attention to her.

"Lauren, I— You—"

"I'll be going now," Anne Santos said. She stood quickly, gave them both a smile and disappeared.

She must have gone out the door, but Lauren couldn't have sworn to it. All she could see was John, standing there in front of her, looking tired, bedraggled and gorgeous.

"These are for you," he said and thrust the roses at her.

She sneezed. "Oh, how nice. I—" She sneezed again. "I—"

"You're allergic to roses."

"Only a little."

He removed them, dropping them outside the door. As he returned, he said, "I should know that."

"It didn't exactly come up." No man had a right to look this good after what he'd been through. The dark shadow of his unshaven jaws only heightened his masculinity. She had to slide her hands under the covers to keep from touching him.

"How are you feeling?" he asked.

"Ridiculous. I don't have any business being here."

"Yeah, right. You were shot in the head. Why would you check into a hospital?"

"I was barely grazed. A Band-Aid would have done the job."

"That's not what your friend, Felix, said. Felix said you could have had a concussion or a skull fracture. He said you were incredibly lucky not to have frostbite, but that you were suffering from exhaustion and hypothermia. He also said a few other things about me that were perfectly justified."

"And just when did you and Felix have this little chat?"

"Last night. I called, you were asleep, but he was around so we talked for a few minutes. He said you're the best ER nurse he's ever seen."

"I'm touched. How come Felix didn't see fit to mention any of this today?"

"He's probably trying to stay out of trouble. Lauren, I'm . . . I'm really sorry."

What she felt at those words was actually sort of interesting. It was possible to go on living after your heart stopped beating. Hers had and here she was, still thinking. Still feeling.

"Sorry for what?" she asked.

It was going to hurt worse than anything and there wasn't a damn thing she could do about it.

"For involving you, for almost getting you killed. When I saw you lying there—" He glanced away quickly. Staring out the window, he said, "I've been scared from time to time, but I've never been as flat-out terrified as I was then."

"It's nice of you to feel that way, but I wasn't anywhere that badly off."

He turned and looked at her, his eyes silvered, his face set. "Nice? Lauren, I am not being nice."

Scratch nice. "Okay, sorry. Does thoughtful work better?"

"Not much." Two quick strides carried him to the side of the bed. He stood there, glowering down at her, looking like an annoyed and somewhat exhausted Greek god. "Maybe I'm not making myself clear. I'm used to feeling responsible for other people. This was different. It occurred to me that if I had to live the rest of my life without you, I'd have a very big problem."

All in all, it was a good thing she wasn't hooked up to a monitor. The funny little skittering beats her heart was making would have had a crash cart unit rolling in right about now.

"P-problem?"

Oh, God, he was serious. He was about to say something, do something and she was totally unprepared. She hadn't resolved anything in her own mind, hadn't even gotten close before his mother walked in. Such a nice woman. Ooops, shouldn't think nice. Maybe the whole Santos family had some sort of aversion to it, although she didn't think so.

"John—?"

"Yes, Lauren?"

"I want you to know something—" She was sliding down the mountain again, going full tilt, the ground falling away beneath her and nothing was left but the long leap into the unknown.

"I'd have a problem, too. I mean living the rest of my life without you. I was thinking that if the subject came up—if it did—I'd have a very hard time making a commitment to a man who lives as dangerous a life as you do. But then I realized that I already had made the commitment."

He looked as though he liked that idea. "When you slept with me?"

"Well, yes, but more so when I followed you off the side of the mountain."

"Hey, if you remember, that was your idea."

"No, the way we did it was mine, but doing it in the first place was yours."

"I'd say it was more Panos's. But what you're telling me is that even though I'm in this really dangerous line of work that you hate, you still think there could be a future for us?"

He was sitting on the bed now, very close. His fingers were stroking her shoulder, playing with the spaghetti strap of her negligee. He didn't look quite so tired anymore.

"There will be a future," Lauren said, a little breathlessly. "The only question really is whether we're going to share it."

"And the answer—"

The answer. Trust John Putnam Santos not to be willing to settle for any nice, safe ambiguity.

She started to reply. He stopped her with a light, tempting kiss that promised a great deal more.

"It might help to know that I love you passionately."

Her eyes widened. The man definitely didn't play fair. "That's, uh—"

"Nice?" He laughed and pressed her back into the pillows, his arms braced on either side of her. She could smell the wind in his hair, the wild scent of hidden places and felt her entire body blaze in response.

In the midst of a blizzard, in the nearness of death, this man was life and hope to her. He made her believe that all things were truly possible.

"I love you, too," she said.

"Are you sure about that?"

"Yes, of course. I'd never say it otherwise."

"Ah, but you see, you fell in love with the dashing man of mystery. Right?"

"I'll give you that."

"How are you going to feel marrying a desk jockey?"

She hadn't heard him right. Marrying? A what?

"Who, uh, you, er…"

"Did I mention that one of the things I love most about you is your articulateness?"

"No, you didn't."

He kissed her then, not lightly but hard and deep, a man claiming reunion with the woman who was the other part of himself. She clung to him, heedless to everything else. Nothing mattered except the moment and the man. The taste, the scent, the feel of him—all engulfed her.

When he moved away finally, they were both breathless.

"What were we talking about?" he asked.

"Desks."

"I'm the new director of drug enforcement for the northeast. Or I will be once the president signs the appointment."

"The president—?"

"He said he'd do that over dinner. Want to come?"

"I don't know. Who's cooking?"

"Some chef, but I promise to be polite. What do you say?"

"To dinner with the president?"

"No, to marriage, commitment, walking off into the sunset together, the whole ball of wax." He hesitated a heartbeat. "There is a catch. The job's based in Boston. I'll commute if that's really what you want, but it's likely to mean a weekend marriage and—"

"Weekend, hell. I expect you every night of the week, John Putnam Santos, or you'd better have one slam-bang excuse."

He kissed her again. Her mouth, her eyes, the curve of her throat. She slid her hands under his coat, tracing the hard lines of his chest and back, loving the power and gentleness of him.

And wishing they were anywhere other than a hospital room where anyone could walk in at any moment. A cave, for instance. That would have been great.

"I want you to promise me something," she said.

"Anything."

Looking into his eyes, she knew that he meant it.

A moment passed before she trusted herself to speak. "Someday we'll go back to that cave. We'll take our kids and camp out."

"Okay, but this time we do it right. If we're going down that mountain again, we're doing it on skis."

"Wait a minute, I never said anything about the mountain. Besides, I don't know how to ski."

"I'll teach you," he said and gathered her close. "And you'll teach me. We'll do it together."

She smiled through the tears that slipped like diamond drops down her cheeks. "John Santos, if there's a man in the world who can get me to go down that damn mountain again, it's you."

Off in the distance, a siren wailed. Neither heard it.

* * * * *

COMING NEXT MONTH

#679 HIDE IN PLAIN SIGHT—Sara Orwig
Heartbreakers
Safeguarding single mom Rebecca Bolen and her two cuddly kids
from a crazed killer was tying Detective Jake Delancy into some
serious knots. He'd had worse assignments, more crafty adversaries,
but he'd *never* before taken his work to heart—or fallen in love....

#680 FIVE KIDS, ONE CHRISTMAS—Terese Ramin
They'd married for the sake of the children, but Helen wanted more.
She *needed* Nat Crockett as surely as any love-struck bride. Only
problem was, Nat didn't seem to share her newlywed notions. But
with mistletoe and five darling matchmakers, Helen vowed to change
his mind.

#681 A MAN TO DIE FOR—Suzanne Brockmann
One minute her life was normal, the next Carrie Brooks was on the
run with a man she hardly knew. Felipe Salazar *was* dangerous, but
he'd somehow captured her trust. And while she knew in her heart
to stand by him, only the face of death revealed the extent of her
devotion.

#682 TOGETHER AGAIN—Laura Parker
Rogues' Gallery
How dare he? Meryl Wallis knew James Brant for the power-hungry
tycoon he was. She'd loved him once, only to be betrayed. Now he
needed her to save his reputation. Well, she had control this time
around—of everything but herself....

#683 THE MOM WHO CAME TO STAY—Nancy Morse
Native American Trace McCall had done his best, but there were
some things he simply couldn't teach his preteen daughter. So
when Jenna Ward took an interest in his parenting dilemma, he
figured there was no harm in letting her "play" a maternal role.
Then he found he wanted her—for real.

#684 THE LAST REAL COWBOY—Becky Barker
Jillian Brandt knew there was no place safer than Trey Langden's
remote ranchland—and rugged embrace. Her enemies were getting
closer, and her life depended on staying out of sight. But hiding
away with her former love posed problems of a very different sort....

MILLION DOLLAR SWEEPSTAKES (III)

EXTRA BONUS PRIZE DRAWING

SWP-S1195

Who needs mistletoe when Santa's Little Helpers are around?

Santa's Little Helpers

brought to you by:

Janet Dailey
Jennifer Greene
Patricia Gardner Evans

This holiday collection has three contemporary stories celebrating the joy of love during Christmas. Featuring a BRAND-NEW story from *New York Times* bestselling author Janet Dailey, this special anthology makes the perfect holiday gift for you or a loved one!

FREE GIFT
with purchase
see inside

You can receive a beautiful 18" goldtone rope necklace—absolutely FREE—with the purchase of *Santa's Little Helpers*. See inside the book for details.

Santa's Little Helpers—a holiday gift you will want to open again and again!

Silhouette®
™

We've got more of the men you love to love in the
Heartbreakers lineup this winter. Among them are
Linda Howard's Zane Mackenzie, a member of
her immensely popular Mackenzie family, and
Jack Ramsey, an *Extra*-special hero.

In December—HIDE IN PLAIN SIGHT, by Sara Orwig:
Detective Jake Delancy was used to dissecting the
criminal mind, not analyzing his own troubled heart.
But Rebecca Bolen and her two cuddly kids had
become so much more than a routine assignment....

In January—TIME AND AGAIN, by Kathryn Jensen,
Intimate Moments Extra: Jack Ramsey had broken
the boundaries of time to seek Kate Fenwick's help.
Only this woman could change the course of their
destinies—and enable them both to love.

In February—MACKENZIE'S PLEASURE,
by Linda Howard: Barrie Lovejoy needed a savior,
and out of the darkness Zane Mackenzie emerged.
He'd brought her to safety, loved her desperately,
yet danger was never more than a heartbeat away—
even as Barrie felt the stirrings of new life growing
within her....

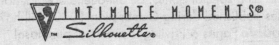

Silhouette

SPECIAL EDITION

CELEBRATION 1000

Nora Roberts

THE PRIDE OF JARED MACKADE
(December 1995)

The MacKade Brothers are back! This month,
Jared MacKade's pride is on the line when he
sets his heart on a woman with a past.

If you liked THE RETURN OF RAFE MACKADE (Silhouette
Intimate Moments #631), you'll love Jared's story. Be on
the lookout for the next book in the series, THE HEART OF
DEVIN MACKADE (Silhouette Intimate Moments #697)
in March 1996—with the last MacKade brother's story,
THE FALL OF SHANE MACKADE, coming in April 1996
from Silhouette Special Edition.

These sexy, trouble-loving men
will be heading out to you in
alternating books from Silhouette
Intimate Moments and Silhouette Special Edition.